Prison Notes of a Woman Activist

Praise for *Prison Notes of a Woman Activist*

'A luminous account of jail from the pen of a sensitive young woman who draws deeply moving sketches of women who sometimes do not even know why they are in prison. Anuradha's stories move from children who are born in prison, with no idea of the world outside their walls – not even knowing what the moon looks like except on television – to old women bent with age serving life sentences and longing for release before they die so that they can die at home. But jail life is also throbbing with humanity in the midst of trauma and sadness. Women share their pain, write petitions for each other, discover histories of the jail where the staff recall other inmates who are incarcerated for their conscience, and unexpectedly the jail library has a copy of one such memoir ... Anuradha is the scribe in the jail, who tells stories of women and children who are victims of a cruel and inhuman world, and the unexpected legacies of kindness, solidarity and courage – women who sustain a spirit of resistance against the cruel norms in the world outside and in the way the law works.

'This is a poignant book about a world we need to know and think about: a world that presses against conventional boundaries and is just beyond the prison walls, not so far from us at all.'

Uma Chakravarti

'Every story compiled in this book has its heart-wrenching moments and all the stories stir different emotions in the reader – anger and helplessness the foremost. Some stories are bound to give you watery eyes ... At the end, some of the questions remain, perhaps unanswered: what is a crime? Who is a criminal? How to make law of the land accessible to hapless common man?'

Suresh Pant

'She is the empathetic sutradhaar who gently navigates the harrowing stories of imprisoned women.'

Priya Ramani (www.BloombergQuint.com)

'B. Anuradha's book takes on the literal meaning of freedom and tries to deconstruct its meaning through several narratives of lives in prison ... This book is not just an account of how life inside a prison has been but is also an attempt to decipher one's own experiences. Thematically the book explores the concept of freedom as one of the strands to understand human nature. Birds that fly in and out of the prison turn into reminders of the captivity of these women.'

Seemen Ali (Sparrowonline.org)

Longlisted for the Valley of Words Award 2022 for translation

Prison Notes of a **Woman Activist**

(TRANSLATED FROM THE TELUGU)

BELLAPU ANURADHA

EDITED BY

GITA RAMASWAMY

ILLUSTRATIONS BY ARUN FERRIERA

RATNA BOOKS

HARPERPERENNIAL

An Imprint of HarperCollins *Publishers*

First published in English in India by Ratna Sagar P. Ltd. 2021
This edition co-published in India in 2026
by
Harper Perennial
An imprint of HarperCollins *Publishers* India
Cyber City, Building 10-A, Gurugram, Haryana-122002, India
www.harpercollins.co.in
and
Ratna Sagar P. Ltd.
Virat Bhavan, Mukherjee Nagar Commercial Complex
Delhi 110009, India
www.ratnabookseries.wordpress.com

2 4 6 8 10 9 7 5 3 1

P-ISBN: 978-93-6989-958-6

Printed and bound at
Nutech Print Services Pvt. Ltd.

FSC
www.fsc.org
MIX
Paper | Supporting responsible forestry
FSC® C195953

This book is printed on FSC® certified paper
which ensures responsible forest management.

HarperCollins *Publishers*, Macken House, 39/40 Mayor Street Upper,
Dublin 1, D01 C9W8, Ireland

Contents

Baby's Day Out

'TODAY IS CHILDREN'S DAY, the day Chacha Nehru was born. Come on, tell me where Chacha Nehru is in these photos?' asked Nirmala, the teacher. The children jumped up to identify Nehru's photo among the seven photos on the wall.

'Very good. Now tell me, who was Chacha Nehru?'

'Sonia Gandhi ka baap (Sonia Gandhi's father),' came Julie's reply promptly. Nirmala spanked Julie and the children laughed.

'Repeat after me – Chacha Nehru was India's first Prime Minister,' said Nirmala. The children repeated it noisily after her.

As Nirmala made an effort to control the unruly children,

Dalo, one of the students, asked her, 'Didi, isn't this Bapu?' pointing at Gandhi's photo. When Nirmala nodded in affirmation, Julie immediately said, 'I know, woh Sanjay Dutt ka baap hai (He is Sanjay Dutt's father).' Nirmala was at her wit's end.

One could not blame these children. Far from recognizing the Father of the Nation or the Prime Minister of the country, these children did not even know what a country means. The only world they had seen so far was within the four walls of the jail. They were prisoners who had not committed any crime and who were not even aware that they were losing their precious childhood in jail. They were the children of women prisoners.

There were about 25 children in Jharkhand's Hazaribagh Central Jail, but Roshni stood out among them.

The day after I entered the jail, four Santhali girls, who were also political prisoners (they were members of a women's organization), asked me to teach them to read. At that time, I did not know Hindi well and within a short period of time I came to know that they spoke and understood the language far better than I did. But they were not too familiar with the script and could not read or write Hindi. Since I had learnt Hindi as a language in school, I could read and write better than them though I could not speak fluently. So, we decided to learn Hindi together and commenced our lessons under a tree. This was when Zubeida Bano came to me along with her five-year-old daughter Roshni and asked me, 'Will you teach us both to read and write?'

Roshni had a round, childish face with soft, short hair that looked like a toupee. She smiled at me shyly. I looked at her and said, 'Come here.' She looked at her mother. As soon as her mother nodded her approval, she came to sit next to me. She held a small school bag made from an old pair of salwar kameez and took out a slate and a book from the bag. It was a picture book titled *Learn ABC* with both Hindi and English text.

I showed her a picture of a dog with the letters 'D' 'O' 'G' written in English and the word 'kutta' written in Hindi next to it and asked her, 'What is this?' She thought for a while and said, 'baagh (tiger)'. I was taken aback. I then showed her a cat's picture and asked her what it was. She immediately identified it as a cat. Then I showed her a tiger's picture and asked her, 'What is this?' Roshni replied, 'Dog.' I looked at Zubeida, confused. Roshni seemed to have sensed that she had made mistakes and her face fell.

Zubeida smiled at me – I can never forget the pathos in that smile. She said, 'I was sent to the Dhanbad jail when Roshni was a month old. My sister-in-law committed suicide by burning herself and I was arrested, along with her husband and another sister-in-law. After two years, they sentenced me to life in prison and I was sent to the Central Jail. Roshni has not seen the outside world since that time. The cat is the only big animal she has ever seen.' I sensed that Roshni was hurt by the surprise in my eyes and did not ask any further questions at that time.

IT WAS EIGHT-THIRTY in the morning. As soon as the bell at the gate rang, all the children ran out with vessels in their hands, shouting 'Doooooodh (milk)...roti.' The children are given two rotis and half a litre of milk. That morning, Roshni came running back to us, placed her rotis on a plate and told her mother, 'Maa, they did not give us milk today.'

Her mother asked, 'Why?'

'I don't know, maybe the milkman's mother did not give milk today.'

This made us all burst into laughter. I asked Roshni, 'Does the milkman's mother give the milk every day?'

'Then whose mother gives the milk?' asked Roshni, innocently.

She did not understand why everybody was laughing. I showed her the picture of a cow in her book and explained where the milk comes from. It was Roshni's turn to be astonished and she kept asking me many questions all through the day.

After some days, two prisoners in our ward were released and Zubeida moved next to me. With this, Roshni and I became even closer friends.

The ward I was housed in was like a large dormitory with seventy prisoners and at least fifteen children. This was the only ward with a television set. The television was not just a form of entertainment, but an addiction for many people in the ward. It was on all the time and it was often difficult for me to put up with the noise.

But when I realized that for children like Roshni, the

television was the only source of knowledge about the outside world, I learnt to tolerate it.

One day, there was a programme on poultry farms on television. I called Roshni and asked her, 'What are those?'

'Murgi (hen).'

'Have you ever seen a hen?' I asked.

'Oh yes!' she said, her eyes shining.

I knew there was no way for her to have seen a hen and asked her, 'Where did you see a murgi?'

She ran up to her mattress, took her book out from underneath it, ran back and showed me the picture of a hen in the book.

I would feel increasingly sad at the way these children were having to spend their childhood. Julie had seen life outside the jail for considerably longer than the other children and knew more about the outside world, which led the other children to admire her. While watching a film, she would explain things to the other children, saying things like, 'This is the hero' or 'That is the villain' or 'This is the heroine'. The other children would listen in awe. I would wonder what I could do for these children but could not figure it out.

Why should children be punished for the crimes their mothers had committed or were accused of having committed? How many of these mothers could leave their children in the care of others? On the other hand, shouldn't a child have the right to stay with its mother?

I asked Zubeida one day, 'Can't Roshni stay outside with her father?' She replied, 'Roshni's father has come to meet me only once since I have been imprisoned. He said he was afraid that he too would be arrested and got scared if he saw the police. I pointed out that his name was not registered in the FIR, but he didn't understand. After they sentenced me, he has practically disappeared. There has been no letter from him or any news. I have since come to know from others in my village that he has remarried. Who should I send Roshni to? Nobody comes to meet me.'

'How long will this continue?' I asked.

'I can keep Roshni with me till she is five years old. She is in her fifth year now. After that, it will continue for as long as they let me. Beyond that, khuda ki marzi (God's will).'

One day, while the children were playing, I heard Roshni say, 'Do you know, we also have a house.' One of the children asked her, 'Where is it?' Roshni told them, 'It is in Dhanbad; we have three big wards in our house.' There was no chance that she could remember anything of the Dhanbad jail. I realized she could only imagine a house in terms of what she was experiencing in Hazaribagh. Like all other children, she also had dreams and an active imagination but these were based on the small world she had seen in the jail. My heart twisted in anguish. If this was my mental state, I could only imagine how her mother must have felt.

One day, Zubeida mentioned something in passing. She said, 'They take the children out once a week in the Dhanbad jail but not in Hazaribagh for some reason.' I did not know there was such a rule. I asked the older inmates about it. They said that earlier the children were taken out once a week even in Hazaribagh but, for some reason, this practice had been stopped. None of them could recall the reason.

We resolved to ask the jail authorities to revive the custom. One day, when the jailor came on his usual rounds, we mentioned this to him along with the other issues we had. As soon as we told him about this, he said that he did remember this practice from when he was a deputy jailor and that he would revive it. He decided to take the children out every Sunday and asked the prisoners to gather all the children who were able to walk and get them ready by 8 a.m.

The children were overjoyed. They came to me every hour with new questions. 'When will they take us? At what time? How? On foot or in the van? Who will come with us? Will our mothers come with us? Will they count us?' Their questions were endless. By the time it was Saturday, they were so worried that the jailor would forget about the trip, that they made me remind the head warder about Sunday's programme. They began tailing me from four in the evening that Saturday. Finally, I approached the warder at the gate. The gang of children followed me. With the children listening to every word of mine, I asked the warder, 'Jailor saab promised these children that he would take them out tomorrow morning. Do remind him about it.'

'Really? I haven't got any orders on this front yet,' he said.

'That is why I am reminding you. Remind the jailor before you leave. Otherwise, the children will be disappointed.' The children grew suspicious at this exchange and the eldest of them, Dalo, stepped forward and told the head warder, 'If you don't take us out, we will not take either chai, doodh or roti or khana.' The rest of the children joined the chorus, shouting, 'Nahin lenge, nahin lenge (we won't accept, we won't accept).' The warder laughed and said, 'See! Under your leadership, the children have also become hardcore agitators.' Julie came forward and told him, 'We will not allow our mothers to eat food.' I laughed and told him, 'Be careful, the children are even beginning to lead us.'

I woke up on Sunday morning to a sound and found Roshni sitting next to me and staring at my face. All the others were asleep, so I raised my brows in enquiry. She whispered, 'Isn't it morning? Why are they not opening the doors? When will the jamadar (head warder) come?'

'It is only four in the morning, go back to sleep,' I told her.

'It is Sunday, isn't it?' she asked, anxiously.

I hushed her and went back to sleep. Poor Roshni. She usually woke up at 7 a.m., and that too only after her mother shouted at her.

As soon as the prisoners were let out of lock-up and counted, all the children rushed out. By the time I was ready for a walk at 6 a.m., they had already bathed and were waiting at the gate. It was only after the escort staff came at 7:30 a.m. and told them, 'All of you, get ready,' that they finally relaxed. At 8 o'clock, the children were lined up and counted. Then, with a female warder and four constables as escorts, they started on their excursion into the outside world.

I was absorbed in reading the day's paper when Roshni ran in, shouting, 'Didi! Didi!' She was carrying a bunch of roses in her hand and came and placed them in front of me, her face flushed with excitement, her lips trembling, her eyes shining like stars. She looked as if she had just returned from a magical land. I was reminded of Alice in Wonderland. It was clear that she desperately wanted to tell me many things, but was out of breath and unable to bring out the words. The other children also came running in after her and began shouting all at once. They dropped the flowers they had brought on my newspaper, dampening it. I poured water in the aluminum plate given to us for our meals and arranged all the flowers.

AFTER ROSHNI RECOVERED, I had her sit next to me and tell me about her excursion. 'What did you see?'

'We went to the talaab (pond), you know. It has water, a lo-o-ot of water. And the water doesn't go anywhere, you know? It stays there. Ah...I saw a goat, you know it just keeps saying 'meh, meh'. I also saw a dog, it was a mad dog.'

'How did you know it was a mad dog?'

'It kept barking at me. I told it to stop barking but it did not listen. It had also applied kaajal (kohl) on its eyes.'

'How could it have done this when it doesn't have hands?'

'Maybe it applied the kaajal with its legs. I saw a pig too and it kept saying 'grr...grr.' She burst out laughing as she remembered the pig.

'We got on the swings in the park there,' she continued. 'Then Didi took us to a temple and asked us to pray. I also prayed to god. I said, 'Shivji, I am a child and I beg you. Give bail to my mother and release all the prisoners.' Then Shivji told me that my mother will get bail and asked me to be happy. There were shiny ribbons tied around the top of the temple. I liked that a lot, you know.'

I asked her, 'Is there anything that you did not like about your trip?' She immediately replied, 'The cycle. It goes very fast and almost ran over us, I was scared. There was a boy on it but he didn't fall, he kept going. I didn't like the cycle. They gave us chocolates too.' She put her hand in her pocket and pulled out some chocolates. She offered me one. 'I don't want it beta, you eat it,' I told her. 'I have more with me, these are really good, eat them,' she said placing a bar of chocolate on my palm.

'Did you see anything else?' I asked her. Her face lit up and she said in an excited voice, 'I saw a trash can!' I crinkled my nose in disgust and said, 'A trash can? That is there in our jail too, why are you so excited about it?'

'That trash can wasn't like the one here. It had so many colourful boxes, papers, plastic bags and other things.' Then she lowered her voice and whispered, 'If you promise not to tell Maa, I will tell you something.'

I nodded.

'Kasam se? Promise?'

'Yes, I promise.'

She continued, 'Dalo and I wanted to go and get some of those. There were even plastic covers, you know. Julie said Didi would scold us if she saw us carrying them. We thought we would hide them in our frocks. When we went to get some things from the bin, the warder saw us and threatened to search us at the gate. If anything was found on us, they would put us in the cells, she warned. Julie told her that small children cannot be put in the cell. But that made Didi even more angry and she said that she would tell our mothers and would not take us out again. So we dropped all those things there and came back,' she concluded, very sadly.

Like *Totto-Chan*,[1] Roshni was discovering and talking about the magical things she had seen in the outside world that day.

As I concluded our conversation and got up, Roshni asked me, without much hope in her voice, 'Didi, tomorrow is not a Sunday, is it?'

– *Translated by* ARAVINDA POTLURI

17 CL (Maoist)

OUT IN SOCIETY, THEY START by asking your name to get to know you. In prison, they ask, 'What's the case?' even before they ask your name. As for me, I used to say, 'Maoist,' because it was easy to understand. No one would understand if I said 'political prisoner'. However, I noticed that when I was introduced to someone, they would refer to me as '17 CL'. I asked another inmate about this. She laughed at my ignorance. 'You've read so much, you still don't know, you are joking!'

But Phoolmuni, who had just walked in, understood that I truly didn't know. This was probably because she was an Adivasi. Educated people like us often find the natives quite innocent. But unlike us, they are not surprised when someone doesn't know something and instead, simply explain it.

'Say there's a 420,' she said, 'That means it's a case of cheating. Do you know what cheating means? It means to swindle someone. Say there is a 302; it is a case of murder. Now, we are a party case; that means 17 CL.'

Sunita interjected, laughing loudly, 'Doesn't Didi know what "cheating" means? Are you teaching Didi English too?'

Phoolmuni was surprised. 'Isn't that a Hindi word?' Phoolmuni would use all sorts of English words, thinking they were Hindi words. Her mother tongue was Mundari.

Later I learnt that what this actually referred to was the Criminal Law Amendment Act. In Jharkhand, Maoist prisoners are booked under this Act. Anyway, wondering if she had referred to 'we' merely casually, I asked her the details of her case.

'I am the same case, Didi,' she said.

Sarita, who was standing next to us, laughed and said, 'No Didi, she's actually the bakra case.' Phoolmuni's face flushed, and she laughed.

I was confused. 'What's this bakra case?' I asked.

'This Sarita is always giving me a hard time,' responded Phoolmuni. 'At first, I explained that it was a bakra case, but no one was able to understand. What did I know? I was tending goats in the woods when they arrested me and brought me in. Then I thought it must be something to do with the goats. For many days, I didn't even know what my case was. While returning from the court one day, a senior officer said, "Seems like you are a 17CL."

"Meaning what?" I asked.

"MCC then?" he said.

"No sir, goat case," I said.

'They all laughed, and asked, "Where's your house?"

'When I told them where I was from, they said, "Oh! That's why!"'

I didn't get any of this, and interjected, 'So where is your house?'

'In the woods,' replied Phoolmuni. 'From a young age, we go into the jungle to collect dry sticks and mahua flowers. If we have goats and buffaloes, we take them to graze. One day, I had taken some goats into the jungle so they could graze. Then the combing police came. A young boy from our village was also with them. The police stopped me and asked him, "Do you know this girl?"

'The boy said, "Yes! I know her."

'"Yes, we belong to the same village," I said.

'That's it. Then they said, "Let's go to the station!"

'I got down on my knees and begged them but they dragged me to the station, saying, "Whatever you are worried about, you'll be on your way in an hour. Let's go!"

'"Master, let me send my goats back!" I pleaded. But no matter what I said, they wouldn't listen. One policeman kept cursing me, and I swear, Didi, not even my father and mother have ever cursed me the way he did. My legs were shaking in fear. But those foul words angered me. I didn't say anything else and went with them. They kept me in the station all night. Next morning, the sub-inspector arrived. He grilled me, asking me the same questions over and over again. They kept me in the station for three more days. On the evening of the fourth day, they put me in a van and brought me to this prison.'

'Didn't anyone from your home come to visit you?'

Tears welled up in her eyes. 'My father is dead,' she said. 'My mother is demented. She keeps wandering away. When I was at home, I did all the work. I fed her, bathed her. I have two brothers – one older, one younger. They both worked as daily wage labourers. Now, one has to take care of mother, one must go to earn wages. For one of them to visit me would mean either there would be no one to tend to my mother, or there would be no one to earn wages. I don't even know if my goats returned home. Who is going to rear them?'

Her grief swelled at these thoughts. She sat there, making no attempt to wipe the tears streaming down her cheeks.

'How long has this gone on?' I asked quietly. Sharing all this lightens the heart.

'Three-and-a-half years. I was arrested in April 2006.'

I noticed that unlike everyone else who said they arrived in say, 'chait' or 'phaghun', she used the English months. So I asked her, 'Did you go to school?'

'I know how to read and write, but didn't go to school,' she said.

Phoolmuni used to attend the sessions held under a tree. She could write faster than the others. Her handwriting was beautiful, so perfect it looked like print. Every day she would keep the newspaper in front of her and practise writing by copying from it. She advised me to do the same.

She was a quick learner. Apparently, she had learnt all the reading and writing she knew in prison through such sessions. Whenever someone who had received some education arrived at the prison, the study sessions would resume. There were books, too. Ultimately, it was only due to Phoolmuni's resoluteness that I, along with the four girls, kept at reading the fifth-grade books and was able to learn Hindi.

ONE DAY, I RECEIVED a letter by post. This created a big sensation. It seemed that until then no one in the women's ward had received a letter by post. No surprise. Those who lived there were either poor or lower middle-class folks. Among them, there were only two or three who were literate or had received any education. If inmates came from nearby villages, their folks would visit them, so there was no necessity to write letters. But the letter which came for me gave Phoolmuni a new idea. She decided to write to her folks.

Before I received my letter, no one knew that the prison officials would bear the mailing charges with government funds. Now, new hope arose inside Phoolmuni. We wrote to her elder brother. We provided detailed instructions about how to get to the prison, what restrictions to be aware of at the outer gate, what kind of identity card to carry, etc. The most important thing that Phoolmuni wanted to convey – and that she stressed thrice in the letter – was, 'Don't be afraid, they won't arrest you.'

After that at least once every day she would come and

start counting the time it would take for the letter to reach her brothers, and the time it would take for them to procure the travel charges. Gradually, her hopes turned into concern, then into anxiety, and ultimately into despair. Several months passed, but no one came to meet her. I felt it was my responsibility to bring her out of her hopelessness.

Quite a few women in the prison used to knit. So I encouraged Phoolmuni to learn knitting. But she didn't have the money to buy knitting needles. What could be done? For breakfast they give us soaked chickpeas. I couldn't eat them. I would give her my share of the chickpeas and instead eat rice that was served at 10 a.m. Likewise I couldn't use the mustard oil we were given for applying on our bodies. So we decided to collect money by selling these.

Because they were inexpensive, a few prisoners would buy them off us and send them home. In this manner, we collected enough money to buy some knitting needles. Phoolmuni picked up the skill quite fast. Quite a few folks there, like members of the security staff or the female warders, would pay and get sweaters, door linings, curtains and shawls knit because these items were expensive in the open market. If something cost two hundred to three hundred rupees outside, they would pay hundred and fifty to two hundred rupees inside. The knitting required a lot of effort.

Phoolmuni began working day and night and quickly rose to the status of taking in orders herself. Prisoners were not allowed to keep more than a hundred rupees with themselves. So the money she made had to be hidden away carefully.

As the earnings began, another thought came up – the money should be used to apply for her bail. As soon as this idea came to me, I ran to her. She jumped up in delight hearing this. But when bail was granted who was to give surety? Disappointment set in again. But let's deal with it when the time comes, I said. She didn't agree. 'If we can't proceed after we do this now, then all this effort will just flow down the river Ganga, isn't it?' she said.

One day there was a visitor for her. She refused to believe it. By the time she returned, a big crowd had gathered at the gate, waiting for a word from her. Isn't that to be expected when, after being in the prison for four-and-a-half years, it is the first time anyone from home visits! As soon as Phoolmuni returned, she sat down among us and broke down crying. While trying to console her, everyone remembered their own families and started weeping. In the end I reproached them, had Phoolmuni drink some water, and then we heard her story.

It seems that once Phoolmuni was imprisoned, her brothers decided to appoint a lawyer. They worked extra hours to earn enough money to pay the lawyer. This meant leaving their mother alone at home. One day, she disappeared. They searched a lot but couldn't find their unstable mother. They had saved up some money by then but were anxious because they didn't know what to do when they received the letter Phoolmuni wrote. They were about to leave when the younger brother developed a high fever. They had to spend all their savings on his treatment, but both his legs were paralysed.

It had taken this long for the elder brother to earn enough money on his own to come visit her. Saying, 'Rest assured, we will get you out, no matter,' he left.

Now that we knew that the letters were reaching their destination, we decided to immediately write another letter addressed to Phoolmuni's brother. We wrote in detail, explaining that there was no need to appoint a lawyer; he just needed to find someone who could stand surety. I had heard a lot about lawyers gouging money like leeches from innocent people. So I spoke to a lawyer I knew, convincing him to argue our case for the one thousand rupees that Phoolmuni had saved, and promising that we would pay him the remaining five hundred after bail was secured. We also found out the phone number of the sarpanch of Phoolmuni's village and arranged for word to be sent to her brother as soon as the bail was granted.

At last, after five years, Phoolmuni, released on bail, went home. Now when I think of Phoolmuni, I wonder, 'Did her goats return home?'

– *Translated by* RAJ KARAMCHEDU

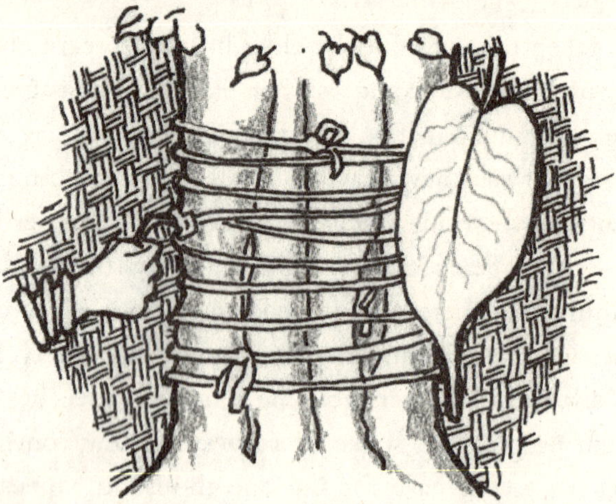

Commerce with the Supernatural!

IT WAS FIVE IN THE EVENING. Birds sat with their mates in a row on the tall prison walls. Chirping and rubbing their beaks, they were engrossed in a conversation we were not privy to, but it was a beautiful sight to behold. Pigeons in the mornings and mynas in the evenings were regular visitors to the prison. They seemed to visit us every day only to remind us of our captivity. One couldn't help but envy them.

The women's barracks was like a jail within a jail. The men – barring the ones in high-security cells – were allowed to move freely inside the jail premises. Women, on the other hand, were confined to their barracks. Every day, during this time of the day, we sat in groups on the L-shaped cement pavement that extended from the gate to the ward and talked to each other. Some of us even walked around in that little space.

The ward was an old, British-era building. In the vacant land on its right, a new building was under construction. On the left, there was a small hospital with four beds and behind it, a single-roomed 'school' for the children of inmates. Bathrooms were located on the left of the open space behind the wards. There was a well on the right and a small, run-down room in the middle. A small patch of soil had been set aside for growing vegetables. This constituted our entire world. The little freedom we were allowed did not last very long. The jamadar (head warder) would come around at a fixed time to send us back into our wards and lock us up.

'If only we could fly away like these birds!' said Reelamala. 'Reelamala' means greenery in Santhali, she told me. What a beautiful name! In Jharkhand, names are close to nature, just like the people.

Out of nowhere, tiny black birds darted above our heads and swooped inside the ward. There were no lights in there. They had probably come looking for their nests in the darkness.

'Haan, new inmates have come!' said Budhini, suddenly.

'There wasn't even the sound of the gates opening. How do you know they are coming?' Reelamala asked.

'On days when birds dart inside like this, we always get new inmates,' said Budhini.

Reelamala and I were both amused by her reply and laughed. 'Birds keep coming in almost every day and new inmates are bound to come. It's a prison, after all,' I said. Budhini wouldn't agree with me at all.

Gita, who had been walking with us and silently listening to our conversation till then, suddenly spoke up. 'I am not sure about the birds, but when the Gayatri Sangh people come and perform bhajans and puja, then new inmates surely come.'

'But they come only once a month, right?' I asked, surprised.

'Yes, Didi,' she whispered, lowering her voice, 'The jail authorities themselves summon them and get them to perform puja so that more inmates come.'

'How do they benefit if the inmates increase in number? In fact, it means more expenditure,' I said.

With a look of pity on her face, she said, 'You're too naïve, Didi. More of us means greater income for them. Why do you think they say "aamad" has come when a new inmate arrives?'

'What does "aamad" mean?' I turned to Reela this time, unable to understand.

'"Aamad" means wealth – you must've heard of "aamdani." Aamdani means income. Aamad is that which gives you aamdani,' Reela explained, in Hindi. I was truly surprised this time. While I knew that prisoners were called 'aamad' here, I had no idea that this was what it meant. Before I could recover from the surprise generated by this new-found information, the bell attached to the gate rang, indicating the arrival of the jamadar. Although I knew that the ring was expected, I jumped with a start on hearing the sound. There was commotion all over the place once again.

'Chalo, chalo! Get inside!' the jamadarin (female warder) went on, rebuking everyone. Some forced themselves to get up, reluctant to move. The jamadarin was relentless, going, 'Chalo…chalo…' as she began prodding us with her lathi.

'Ei, Didi! If by any chance you are fired from this job, you can survive by tending livestock. You will be really good at it!' said a convicted inmate, crushing the khaini (tobacco) in the palm of her left hand with her right thumb.

'You are always obsessed with getting me fired!' the jamadarin smiled, gently rapping her on the head with her knuckles.

'When you go to the forest to tend your goats, they will catch hold of you and shove you into a jail claiming you are a Maoist – just like they did to me,' said Phoolmuni. Everyone laughed.

Phoolmuni had been apprehended by the combing police while she was in the forest grazing her goats. 'We'll conduct a brief inquiry and send you back immediately. Come to the police station with us!' they had told her. They detained her in the station for four days and sent her to jail later. Three years had passed since. 'I hope my goats got home safely,' Phoolmuni kept wishing mournfully.

There was the sound of the gate opening and knowing that we couldn't put it off anymore, all of us dragged ourselves into our ward that resembled a stable. We were like goats or pigs being herded inside in the evening. A few looked towards the west, paid obeisance to the sun probably, and on their way in, bowed to the door. Thinking I must ask them when I get the chance why they bowed to the door like that, I too walked in.

Our ward was a large hall, divided into two parts. This was the largest among the three wards in the Hazaribagh jail. In each of the two parts, there were two rows of beddings from end to end. I went to the spot allotted to me, spread my bedding, and sat down. Everyone was settling down noisily in their spots. The pahara (guard) came and rebuked us, 'Abey! Sit down, everyone!'

Hearing the sound of boots, those of us who had not spread their beddings yet also sat down at once. The jamadar came in, did the headcount, and as he was about to leave, turned to the female guard and declared, 'Seventy-four!'

'Ji saab!' she said, nodding her head.

The headcount done with, he shut the doors, locked them, and after pulling the lock once to check if it was secure, moved onto the next ward.

As soon as he left, the clamour resumed. A woman switched on the television immediately. Nothing could be heard in that din, so she turned up the volume to the maximum. Railway stations and fish markets were no match for our ward.

I sat cross-legged on my five-and-a-half feet bedding and opened a book. Putting up with the commotion was very difficult. Only by diving into the world of books and shutting your ears and mind to the world around can you make the chaos disappear.

Before I could even open the book and attempt to read, Somri came up to me. A convicted prisoner, she had been in this jail for sixteen years. Moving her hands swiftly, she was trying to convey something to me in a particular variety of Hindi infused with Santhali. My limited knowledge of Hindi was of no help in understanding her, so I asked Reelamala to translate.

After listening intently to what Somri had to say, Reelamala smiled, turned towards me, and said, 'Didi! Somri says she feels like she has to take a dump every time she eats something. She wants to know why this is happening, when clearly this isn't normal.'

'Maybe the food isn't getting digested. Is her stomach hurting too?'

Even as I asked this, Somri interrupted me and gesticulating wildly before my face, said as if letting me in on a secret, 'You know? She was staring at me all the while I was eating. I knew it then itself. That she cast an evil eye on me.'

This time, I managed to understand nearly half of her words. 'Who cast an evil eye on you?' I asked, smiling.

Somri was sombre. 'This isn't a joke. Not funny. It's for real! That new inmate, Kamli…it is her!' she said, tagging an expletive to her name. 'She is a daayan, a witch, you know?' After tormenting us with her babble for another half hour, she left us to enquire about the state of affairs in a group engaged in loud brawling. We felt relieved.

'People from this region are very superstitious. They ascribe supernatural causes to every possible problem. This might seem surprising to you,' said Reelamala, smiling.

'You are more of a surprise to me than that. You, too, were born in this state. That too, in a village that is far more backward than the rest. How then did you end up becoming a revolutionary who believes none of these things, I wonder.'

'True! I was educated during my time in the party. There were constant debates and campaigns against superstitions. The cultural teams, in particular, were engaged in this. I began to understand these matters gradually. The fact that I am a second-generation party member may also have helped. My father was a kisan committee leader. My mother was an activist in the women's organization. Growing up in that political milieu made it a little easier for me to grasp things. To this day, new entrants to the party and those who haven't been there for long, have a residue of such notions left in them. I...'

Before she could finish, loud wailing sounds arose from the brawling group. We couldn't hear each other in that maelstrom of voices and I sat there holding my head in my hands. Reelamala stood up and went towards the crowd to find out what had happened.

Just then, Basanti emerged from the crowd, cursing loudly. Reelamala asked her what the matter was. 'If that whore shoves the money inside her sari and moves around, will it stay put there?' she said. From her barrage of expletives, we gathered that Kamli had lost the five-hundred-rupee note she had hidden in the folds of her sari. Afraid that someone might steal it, she had hidden it there. She kept pulling it out repeatedly and checking it, apparently. It seemed to have slipped off somewhere and was now missing.

Everyone was now coming up with their own list of suspects. Weeping, Kamli had been going around the ward asking, 'Oye Didi, if someone has taken my money, return it. I won't call anyone a thief. I will bow down at your feet. Give a poor woman's money back!' After going around like this several times, she returned to her spot and started crying again.

Someone gave her some brilliant advice – offer a reward of fifty rupees to whoever returns it. Once again, Kamli desperately went around the whole ward with this proposal. Rinku, who liked bossing around, was stirred into action. She began investigating, asking questions like who had sat near Kamli, and started issuing threats. If someone unwittingly got caught, she probably intended to extort half of the amount from them. She had considerable experience in such matters.

This was when something unexpected happened. Kamli wiped her tears after crying for a while. Her hair had come loose, falling all over her shoulders, and her eyes had turned red. She addressed everyone in the ward in a ringing voice, 'Listen, everyone!' Slowly, the entire ward fell silent. 'All of you must know I am a bhaktin, a woman supposedly capable of performing magic. I give you a night's time. Put the money back where you took it from by dawn. I will do jhaadphook (black magic) tonight. If you don't give it back, you will vomit blood till you die!' she said, lashing her hair like a whip and then tying it up. She tied her hair up, went and washed her hands and feet, came back and put kumkum on the wall next to her bedding. After that, she closed her eyes and began to mumble something. Opening her eyes after some time she said, 'I know I will get my money back in the morning.'

Once more, there was unrest all over. Everyone had their own take on what had transpired. They started swapping tales about the jhaadphook-induced deaths they knew of. Realizing that reading was now impossible, I put my book away and started talking to Reelamala. Inevitably, our conversation turned towards superstitions. I remembered reading about how, when the Communist Party of the Philippines had first formed its armed troops, the CIA had used such superstitions and unfounded fears to destroy the party's armed troops and caused serious damage to the movement. I told Reelamala about this.

'How did they manage something like that?' asked Reelamala, evincing interest.

'First, they spread rumors that a vampire was on the prowl in the region'

'What's a vampire?'

Explaining a vampire in my half-cooked Hindi proved to be quite difficult. Yet, somehow I managed.

'Like the dragons of the Chinese, vampires too are mythical creatures. But the vampire is a kind of a bird, believed to bite the necks of humans and drink their blood. Once, when the troops were crossing the borders of the forest, the CIA suddenly and noiselessly attacked the last person in the line, stifled him, and dragged him away. Then, they pierced holes in his neck and hung him upside down from a tree. They waited till all the blood trickled out of his body and the next morning, flung his corpse outside the village.'

'Abba, how cruel!' remarked Reelamala, flinching.

'Imagine what kind of panic this must have caused in a place like that,' I said.

Reelamala remained silent for a few seconds.

'How did you carry on your work among people who are so superstitious? I guess the party too must have had a tough time here,' I asked her.

'I do not know what challenges the party faced when it started its work in these parts,' she replied, 'But now, the movement has become strong. We spread our message through cultural programmes. Although superstitions are far from becoming extinct, the party is able to use the situation to its advantage with people's cooperation. People inside the government are also equally superstitious, right?

'Once, a reporter questioned Shibu Soren about the political instability in the state and asked him what he would do about it if he came to power. Do you know what his reply was? "There is a problem of vaastu in the Assembly building. I will modify it." When asked, "Then what is your strategy to come to power?" he said, "I will organize shanti pujas". These are the opinions of the leader of a major political party like the Jharkhand Mukti Morcha, which professes that it will put Jharkhand on the path of progress!'

This was true. I had read that interview too. I began to ask her, 'What about the party's experience with…'

Before I could complete my question, Reelamala

interjected, 'You know what happened once?' and started laughing, probably recollecting the incident she was about to relate. I looked at her with interest. Stifling her laughter, pushing back the curly hair falling on her forehead and with a sparkle in her eyes, Reelamala began speaking.

'Once, we had set up camp for a meeting when we were informed that the police were patrolling the area as part of a combing operation. We didn't have much time. Shifting our camp meant two days of journey, and the leaders felt that it was better not to risk it. The commander mulled over it and gave a suggestion. "Let us call the kisan committee leader, Kanuda, from the nearby village and talk to him. He is everyone's favourite. It would be better to know his opinion before taking a decision."

'When he broached the matter with Kanuda, he confirmed that the police were indeed patrolling the area and were likely to find us. This got us thinking again and we wondered if we were taking a risk by staying put. Then, an old man who was accompanying Kanuda said, "The police won't come this way. Even if they do, we'll ensure they don't cross the peepal tree and come this way."

'When asked what he would do, he said, "I will cast a magical spell." Kanuda laughed at the idea saying, "You can't get magic to drop raw tamarinds!"

'"But I can get the police to stop," said the old man seriously.

'The old man was not someone who indulged in empty talk. He meant business. Besides, he was well-respected by everyone in the village. Everyone paid heed to his words.

Leader comrades consulted separately with the old man and discussed everything in detail. It was then decided that we should carry on with our meeting.'

'Did the police come?' I interrupted, unable to contain myself.

A smile bloomed on Reela's lips. 'Oh yes, they did,' she said, 'The peepal tree that the old man mentioned was on the outskirts of the village. He called a meeting of everyone in the village and gave them instructions. They smeared the peepal tree with vermillion. Mouli dhaaga, the red-coloured thread, was tied to it. They wrapped a red cloth around its trunk and began to worship it.

'The police did come, as predicted. It was a dense forest beyond the peepal tree. If you didn't know the area too well, finding your way at night wasn't very easy. As soon as the police arrived, they woke up all the people in the outlying houses and asked them to come and show them the way into the forest. The villagers went and brought the old man. The old man said to the police, "Oh! How can we go into the forest, when crossing the peepal tree itself is out of the question?" The police were taken aback. The old man told the police that recently a villager had been possessed. In an effort to curb the spirit, they had cast a spell on the man and ultimately exorcised and tied the evil spirit to the peepal tree. If anyone crossed the tree at night, they would vomit blood until they died. The old man insisted that even speaking about the spirit at night was forbidden and burst into a song, apparently intended to drive evil spirits away.'

'Were they convinced?' I asked, with surprise.

'Convinced? They ran away so fast that they never returned to that area. What's more, three or four of the policemen were so scared they got diarrhoea.'

I too joined her laughter.

'But, do you think the money will be found?' I asked her.

'No doubt whatsoever. You will see tomorrow!' she said.

EIGHT IN THE MORNING, Reelamala and I were sitting beneath the jackfruit tree, reading the papers. All of a sudden, she burst into laughter. I peeked into her paper to find out what was so funny.

Arjun Munda, who was to be sworn in as the new chief minister, was asked by the reporters: 'You wore a red half-coat when you took oath in your last two terms. Will you be wearing it this time as well? It proved quite lucky for you!'

This was the front-page news in Hindustan Times. 'After two years of President's Rule and so much political turmoil, they had nothing else to ask except that! That's Jharkhand for you!' Reelamala quipped.

This is why I was so fond of her. For someone who had never been beyond the forest, Reelamala could surprise me with comments like these. My respect for revolutionary politics, which created such awareness, went up.

In the meantime, a commotion had arisen in the backyard. Everyone started running towards the noise. Anxious to find out what had happened, Reelamala and I also ran, our hearts beating heavily. The five-hundred-rupee note had been found lying among the plants behind the bathrooms.

Who was the first to spot it? The investigation had started. 'Anand ki mayya (Anand's mother),' said someone. If an inmate's child accompanied her to the prison, she was always referred to as the child's mother. Calling her by her name was out of the question.

The kamanis (convicted inmates who have to do hard labour) had unleashed a torrent of expletives. 'We cleaned the drains just now. We would've spotted it, had it been lying there for a while. She must've thrown it just now.' There was some truth to their claims.

'You are accusing me of stealing it just because I showed it to all of you?' said Anand ki mayya in response and launched her counter-attack, hurling invectives at them. Unable to stand the expletives any more, we returned to our spot.

Letting her hair loose, holding the note in her joined palms, and trembling as if in a trance, Kamli walked past us.

We remained seated beneath the jackfruit tree, reading a newspaper each, oblivious to her antics. We finished reading and lifted our heads to find a huge crowd gathered near the hospital's staircase. Wondering what fresh mayhem had erupted, we went there.

Kamli was sitting regally on the highest step. A woman was pressing her feet and asking, 'When will I get bail?' Behind her, many people were awaiting their turn and jostling each other. As Kamli cast chickpeas on the raised platform and read her fellow inmates' fortunes, we stood there speechless.

– *Translated by* Aditya K.

Dheesaali (Courageous Woman)

NONE OF MY JAILMATES ever said anything good about Durga. In jail, if you hear that someone is a good person, it is usually true, but if you hear that someone is a bad person it might not be true. This is more the case with female prisoners. I can't say I knew this earlier, because I realized it only a day before Durga was released.

All the jail inmates had only one thing to say about Durga: 'Don't ever get in her way. Remember, she hacked someone to death in broad daylight and came to jail.' This is how she was always introduced. She was always surrounded by five or six people. Everyone called them the 'Durga gang'.

Earlier, in the Hazaribagh jail, there was only one water tank in the women's ward. All hundred of us had to take our water from this tank. Actually it should not have been difficult to take one or two buckets of water for each one because it was only for drinking. For washing clothes and other needs, we had to draw water from the well. But some inmates did not like well water or felt that it was too laborious a task and started storing tank water in cans to use for their washing. From then on, street-fighting scenes – which we see around village taps in drought areas – became part of our everyday life. It was in this kind of a scenario that I saw Durga for the first time.

Every evening, just before lock-up, we used to keep our cans and pots in a row in front of the water tank. In the morning, as soon as the lock was opened, everyone would run towards the water tank. What started as small face-offs invariably ended up as major fights.

I think that it was either on the second or third day after my arrival that the following incident happened. At that time I didn't have any luggage of my own, and so I was using things belonging to the other political prisoners. Just as I was going to fill my can, Lalita came running up to me, shouting, 'Didi! Didi! Don't go!' Her shouts startled me so much that I dropped the can and stood there like a guilty person. 'What happened?' I asked Lalita in a voice full of fear.

'Baap re…how can you manage with that gang! After the Durga Gang goes away, the two of us can go collect water,' she said. I did not understand. I simply said, 'What can they do to us? We will also stand in the queue and collect water.' She looked at me as if I was a very naive person. 'You don't know anything, Didi,' was her response. Feeling too awkward to ask any further questions, I simply stood in one corner, watching the ongoing water fights. At that time I didn't know much Hindi, but I could still understand that they were abusing each other.

Into that war zone entered Durga, fearlessly, with her buckets and followers. Half the people made way for her. I did not understand if it was fear or respect that they were displaying. It took a long time for me to understand what it was and why those women moved in a gang.

I was curious about what was going on near the tap but could not make out anything. After some time, she emerged from the crowd with buckets full of water, followed by her friends. I didn't pay much attention to her. Later that same evening, after lock-up, when we were all sprawling on our bistars (bedrolls) in our places, chattering away noisily, I heard a voice above the din, saying, 'Pranaam, Didi.' Someone sitting near the entrance was raising both her hands above her head in salutation to me. In answer to my surprise, the prisoner beside me leaned over and said, 'Didi, that is for you only…that is Durga.' Nothing could be heard in that cacophony. So I simply waved my hand. All this seemed a bit dramatic to me. Before I could say anything she said, 'Durga hacked someone to death in broad daylight. She has been given life imprisonment.' I nodded to indicate that I already knew this. 'Maybe she has come to know now that you are here on a party-related case,' said my neighbour. 'That might be the reason…!' I simply shrugged. 'That means she considers you a friend,' laughed Lalita who was sitting on the other side.

Soon after, I started going to court regularly as one or the other new case kept being filed against me. As a result, I didn't have much time to get acquainted with all the inmates. However, as it was a small world that we were living in, I often bumped into Durga. Whenever we came face to face, we exchanged smiles.

Every morning, two or three vans came to the jail to take prisoners to court. There were separate lock-up rooms for men and women within the court premises. We were kept there till evening. Whoever was called to appear before the judge was taken inside and after they were done, brought back to the lock-up. If someone was arrested in the evening, they too were brought to the lock-up room after being produced before the magistrate. Later, all of us returned to the jail together.

One day, when I was in the court lock-up, waiting to appear before the judge, the police brought in three new women. Two of them were very old, while one was young. You could see poverty writ large on their faces. They were clearly very afraid of courts and police stations. Seeing the small lock-up room, they became even more frightened and started weeping loudly.

I tried to console them. The younger one was looking at all of us wide-eyed and asking, 'Do we have to stay here? Is this a jail?' She was so stricken with grief that she couldn't even speak properly. I told them that this was not the jail and that we would all go to the jail soon and there would be many more people in the lock-up over there. She looked at me in disbelief. I gave her my bottle of water and told her to drink some water and not worry. The girl took the bottle with hesitation. Only after I assured her that it was okay to drink from my bottle, did she take a small sip of water.

One of the old ladies lifted both her hands towards me in namaskar to show her gratitude. She asked me if I worked there. She thought I was an employee. 'Why do you salute me? I too am a prisoner here,' I told her.

This time, all three of them looked at me with surprise. 'Then will you be with us in jail?' the young woman asked me, with hope in her voice. 'Yes, all of us will be there together,' I said. By then, they had recovered a little, particularly the young one. But grief seemed to be stuck permanently on the faces of the older women.

After we reached the gate of the women's ward in the jail, they were told to stand apart from the rest of us because they were new prisoners. When she saw me going inside, the young woman looked like a frightened deer. I decided to wait for them. She was so scared that she could not answer the jamadarin's (female warder's) questions. When she was asked her father's name, she answered, 'Budeshwar Paswan.'

As soon as she heard this, Durga, who was standing at a distance, talking to someone, came over and stood beside the jamadarin. After the formalities were over, she called the three women aside, telling the jamadarin that they were her people. When they looked at the stranger with surprise, she said, 'Chalo, bahin (let's go, sister),' to the young woman, and 'Chalo, mayya (let us go, mother)' to the older women and took them inside. I thought that they must be from the same place and headed to my ward.

The next day, Durga came and spoke to me in a very friendly manner. She said that she had a *mulaqaat*,[2] and gave me some sweets. Today she was meeting someone from home.

One day, news broke out that Durga was soon going to be released. It spread like wildfire across the wards. For the next few days, we kept hearing something or the other about her release. But as I was busy attending court or giving the children their lessons, I did not pay much attention.

One Sunday, we were all relatively free. I had washed my hair and as I was feeling a little cold, covered myself with a shawl. After finding myself a sunny spot, I settled down with a book. Almost all the inmates were sitting around in groups, talking and enjoying the sun.

Then Durga came. She too seemed to have washed her hair. Her thick curly hair fell on her face. She had tied a rubber band around it and left it loose. It completely covered her back, and was flying about due to the breeze. She was neither tall nor short, neither dark nor fair. She wore a large bindi on her forehead and had smeared vermillion thickly along the parting of her hair. Her eyes were lined with kohl and she wore big studs in her ears and a nose ring on one side of her nose. You could make out that she had worn her sari with a lot of care, as the pleats were neatly arranged. She also wore a sleeveless red woollen jacket over her blouse. She had red and green bangles on her wrists. I don't remember observing her so carefully earlier. She looked dressed up for a special occasion. Her face was glowing with happiness.

She came up to me and said, 'Didi…I hope I am not disturbing you?' I moved to one side and invited her to sit down.

'Didi, I am going to be released soon, most probably tomorrow or the day after tomorrow.'

'I am very happy to hear this. How long have you been in jail?' I asked.

'A few days short of 10 years.'

'Really? I heard you were given life imprisonment,' I said, a little surprised.

'True, what you heard is right. I was given life imprisonment. You must have heard about the whole case. It was a murder case. It took place in broad daylight.' She was smiling as she spoke, as if she was talking about casual things.

'Yes, I heard about it when the others were talking.'

'What did you hear?' she asked, laughing.

'That…you killed someone with an axe.' I said, a little hesitantly.

This time she laughed out loud. 'That is how rumours spread in jail,' she said, shaking her head. 'Anyway, it is not their fault,' she continued, 'I never told anyone the details either. Sometimes, it is good that stories like these are spread about us. But I want to tell you my story. In fact, I wanted to tell you as soon as I came to know that you were here on a party case. I had wanted to tell you even on the day when you comforted Paswan Chachi (aunt). She likes you very much. I feel you are a good person; that is why I want to tell you my story.

'I am from the Chamar caste. My husband studied a little, maybe till the fifth or sixth grade. But he is very intelligent. He had good friends and got contractual jobs through them. He was earning quite well by the grace of god. We have three children. We were keen on educating them well. We sent them to school. I also did odd jobs. Gradually, we saved some money, sold the little land we had, and shifted to the town for the children's education. We found a small plot in a good area and built a house there.

'Our neighbours belonged to the dominant caste. They didn't like us living next door. Every day, the woman would abuse us from morning to evening on any pretext. Initially, we didn't understand that she was abusing us. Afterwards she started abusing us directly. She made our life miserable. Every day, she picked a new fight, so much so that our children couldn't study in peace. They became very disturbed. Sometimes, she used to abuse our caste. My children were studying hard, Didi. But they failed their exams because of this. The atmosphere at home was hellish. But where could we go? And why should we go?

'One day, her abuse began very early in the morning and went on for a long time. It was almost eleven. Then you know what she said? She said, "You beef-eating bitch! Why eat only the meat of dead animals? Slaughter your son, he looks like an animal, and eat his meat!"

'My blood boiled. I couldn't control myself. Taking a wooden pestle, I went up to her, grabbed her by her hair, and dragged her to the road. Then I hit her with the pestle. Believe it or not, I hit her only once, Didi. She fell to the ground and never got up. Dropping the wooden pestle, I warned all my neighbours, "From today onwards if any of you even glances in my direction or that of my children, I will chop you up." Then, I locked my house and took my children to my mother's place. For four days, I waited for the police to come. But they didn't. On the fourth day, I went to work after sending my children to school.

'That day the police came and asked for me. My mother told them that I had gone to work. But they didn't come to my workplace. Later, I went to the police station myself, fearing that they might trouble my mother. I went directly to the Circle Inspector and said, "Bada babu, you can write what you want. I killed that woman with one blow in broad daylight in the middle of the road. File whatever case you want." He was stunned and remained speechless for a while. Then he arrested me and sent me to jail.

'I told my children and husband not to shed a single tear. I told them, "I live like a tiger, I am going to the jail like a tiger. You too should live like a tiger's children. I will come out exactly after fourteen years. If anyone gives you any trouble, I will see the end of them as soon as I come out. Meanwhile, you should study hard." Then I left my children in my sister-in-law's custody. I told my husband to give them money regularly.'

As Durga continued her story, many things became clear. The girls in her 'gang' felt protected in her presence as they too were dalits. Durga was trying to help dalit prisoners all along. That is why she had come and stood beside the jamadarin the day Paswan Chachi came to jail. I understood that Durga had realized they were dalits and had come to stand by them! My admiration for her grew in the course of our conversation. It was quite clear now why the others gave way to Durga when she went to fill water.

'On the day when the charge sheet was filed against me in the court, the judge asked me if I would like to confess to my crime. I said, "Look, sir, I didn't intend to kill her. But she died because I hit her. Give me whatever punishment you want to." My advocate looked at me aghast. I was given life imprisonment.

'Since it has been almost ten years into my sentence, my husband went to the High Court for a review. This time, he caught hold of a big lawyer. That lawyer argued in court saying that my crime had been committed in a fit of anger and that I had admitted it was a mistake. He pointed out that I had saved the court time by admitting to the crime. Since I had hit her only with a wooden pestle, he argued that I did not have the intention to kill. He raised many points like this, it seems. Eventually, the judge asked for a written undertaking from me, stating that I repented what I did. My husband and the advocate came to visit me in jail to tell me about the judge's instructions. I told them that I won't do it. But my husband pleaded with me to think about our children and started crying. I felt sorry for him and put my thumb impression on the application. Now, the High Court has given the order for my release. Once the order reaches the jail, they will release me.

'All my friends here feel bad that I am leaving them. But how can I be here forever? We stay here like one family. We eat together, move together. That is our real strength. What does it matter whether I am here or elsewhere! Why did I do what I did? Because I wanted to live with my head held high. Didi, tell me did I do anything wrong?'

In her eyes was the confidence that she did not expect an answer.

– *Translated by* RIGOBERTHA PRABHATHA

The Real Jail

'EKSAUBAARAH (112)...EKSAUTERAH (113)...'

I waited till she finished counting the coins and placing them in her box and asked her with a smile, 'Will you teach me to count in Hindi?' She looked embarrassed, quickly put her money box aside, adjusted the bedsheet on the mattress, and said, 'Oh Didi, it's you! Please come.'

I looked at her friendly face and introduced myself as a new inmate of the prison. When I was about to tell her my name, she interrupted me and said, 'I know, Didi. In fact, I was thinking of coming to you to introduce myself. I am Sunita Singh.'

'You run a school here, I understand?' I asked her. 'Will you teach me Hindi? I am not good at it; I thought maybe I could learn the language from you.'

'Baap re!' she exclaimed, 'I should teach you Hindi? I heard that you are well educated. I read a lot about you in the newspapers.'

'Oh! That is all a media creation! I am just a graduate and passed Hindi with the bare minimum marks in the tenth class. As you can see, I struggle to speak Hindi and most people do not understand what I say. I am especially bad at counting in Hindi. When I heard you counting...'

Before I completed the sentence, she said, 'I am trying to count the number of sweaters I knit.'

When I looked at her quizzically, she held her money box up and said, 'Do you know what this is? This is the count of the sweaters that I have knitted here. I do it to pass time, not for money – I have enough of that. Initially, I did not want to take money, but no one does anything in this jail without payment, so I too started charging one rupee per sweater. This way, I have a count of the number of sweaters I have made. My husband keeps taunting me that this is all useless work.' Even while talking to me, she had picked up her needles and started knitting.

I was amazed at the speed with which the needles moved in her expert hands and said, 'It is a good way to pass the time, isn't it?'

'True, this helps me pass my time, but sometimes I feel as if I am harnessing all my strength and pushing at this infinite time in front of me,' she replied, in a dejected tone. She quickly recovered and said, 'Oh, you asked me to teach you Hindi and here I am talking about all manner of things. Fine, I will definitely teach you Hindi. Come over whenever you can.'

Our meeting that day slowly progressed into friendship over time. We got to know each other well. Sunita was born into a rich Rajput family in Bihar. She was the eldest daughter-in-law in her husband's home, a joint family. Her devrani, that is, her brother-in-law's wife, had committed suicide by hanging herself. Her devrani's family filed a case accusing Sunita, her husband, her father-in-law, and her son of being complicit in the death. The accusation was that Sunita and her son had killed her devrani and hung her from the fan while her husband and father-in-law watched without stopping them. The father-in-law took the advice of their family lawyer and sent her away to another village fearing that the family would lose its reputation if the daughter-in-law were sent to jail. The others were arrested by the police.

They were all able to get bail thanks to the influence her father-in-law had. For two years, Sunita lived a secret life away from her family. It was not really such a secret, but the police had been given bribes so they would willingly ignore the fact. Meanwhile, the other three were tried separately and acquitted. This gave her family the courage to have Sunita surrender in court. They believed that she too would be acquitted. That's how she ended up in jail. Not only did she not get bail from the lower courts, even the higher court denied her bail. The family spent an enormous amount of money to get the case heard expeditiously. The other girl's family was no less powerful. In a most unexpected turn of events, she was sentenced to ten years of imprisonment. Following this, she was moved from the district jail to the central jail. She appealed to the high court, claiming that she was innocent and had been wrongly sentenced by the lower courts. The appeal had been admitted and she had applied for bail again. This is where things stood, from what I gathered from her.

I used to walk around in the jail regularly both in the morning and in the evening. Since there was little scope for any kind of physical work, it was necessary for me to walk. There were probably ten or fifteen inmates who used to walk every day. Sunita too had the habit of walking. Interestingly, she always carried a ball of wool in her pocket and would knit even while walking. It was rare to see her without wool and without knitting.

There was a school in the jail for children who were incarcerated along with their parents. Sunita was given the responsibility of running the school. Convicted inmates in the jail are assigned work and given wages for the work. Though the wages are very low, those who work are given a remission – every nine months that they work in jail is considered as twelve months of jail time. I gathered all this information from Sunita. Since Sunita was educated, she was seen as a good fit for the school. However, she did not run it. When I asked her why, she said, 'I do not have the temperament to teach. I cannot take up any work that needs me to use my brain. I am being pressurized to take up this responsibility.' I told her, 'This is a good use of your time. Take me in as your student as well. It is a good timepass for us and good for the children.' She was very pleased and said, 'Will you join the school? If you do, I will start the lessons.'

Sunita was very devout. I noticed that many people became very devout after they entered the jail. Sunita used to bathe early in the morning and perform various rituals and puja. She would not even drink tea before her ablutions and puja. After completing all the rituals and her breakfast, she used to run the school from noon till three in the afternoon, with a ten-minute tea break at one-thirty in the afternoon.

During one such break, I was humming a tune to myself. It was winter and the sun felt very pleasant. We were all covered in shawls and enjoying our tea. I did not notice but the children became silent as if to hear me sing. Sunita looked at me and insisted that I sing louder. The children joined her and began shouting in chorus, demanding, 'Sing a song, sing a song.' I said, 'Let's form two groups and play antyakshari, a game in which one has to sing a song starting with the last letter of the song sung by the previous person.'

Sunita participated enthusiastically. She had a good voice. I asked her, 'You have such a good voice, why don't you sing more freely?'

She smiled and said, 'I feel shy; someone might hear me sing.'

'So what?' I persisted. 'This is a women's ward. Even if someone hears you, it will be a woman. Why then are you so reticent?'

Her face changed colour. 'True Didi, there is no one here, and still I feel scared. In my in-laws' home, there is nothing worse than a woman singing. We are not even supposed to laugh. We are supposed to walk silently, never to be seen without the ghoonghat or veil. We need to ensure that it is drawn properly over our heads all the time. No matter what we are doing – whether cooking meals, or taking care of children – our biggest concern is whether the ghoonghat is covering our heads properly!' She continued, 'When I came here, people used to laugh at me for keeping my head covered. Now I realize that there is more freedom inside the jail! No one to worry about, no one to answer to.'

'How did you complete your studies then?' I asked her, surprised.

'In my mother's home, they were not very particular about such customs. I used to go to college while staying with my brother in Delhi and learnt to drive a two-wheeler. I used to wear salwar-kameez. Since my father had a job with the central government, we had mostly lived in towns. My husband saw me at a wedding and liked me. When the proposal came, I was not very open to it since he is dark. But I agreed to marry him after I spoke to him.' While she was narrating how she met her husband, I could see her cheeks turn crimson.

Sunita was not very fair; she had a wheatish complexion. However, her cheeks and her eyelids were pink. Initially, I had mistakenly thought that it was because she wore make-up and would get irritated, wondering why anyone would do so in jail. I remember the way she used to dress up in heavy and expensive saris, with the end covering her head, and vermillion on the parting of her hair, and the way she used to walk around with a brass plate full of puja paraphernalia. She looked like a rich daughter-in-law in a high-budget television series! It was a surreal spectacle – the high walls of the jail, the barricaded iron gates, poverty everywhere, and this rich, traditionally attired married woman!

When I was first brought to the jail, I thought we would all be given white saris to wear; this is what we see in the movies. But that was not the case. Only those serving sentences are given uniforms by the government. Men are given white uniforms, women are given regular saris. During festivals such as Dussehra and Holi too, women are given saris.

I asked her if her husband was also conservative. She replied, 'I am happy that he is not so traditional, but he is scared of his father and always bound by his word. He will never speak up in front of his father. I used to wear nighties in our bedroom, but whenever I needed to step out of the bedroom I had to put on a sari.'

She continued, 'Once, I wanted my husband to buy me a sleeveless nightie I had seen in the market, but my husband worried that his father might see it when I hung it outside to dry! He is such a coward!' Her face was full of disdain as she said this. 'That's how my domestic life was,' she rued. 'There was no pleasure in it. I was scared to even sing in my own bedroom. My husband is even more scared than I am. You know, Didi, we need to take my father-in-law's permission even if we want to go shopping. If he denies permission, we have to get back inside the house.'

She continued, 'There is no difference between home and jail. The only difference is that I have my children and my husband around me at home. I am at least spared the presence of my father-in-law in jail and don't have to worry about my ghoonghat, except when performing puja. I once asked my husband when he came to meet me in jail to bring me some nighties. He made light of my request and did not bring them. So I got mad with him and requested the jail jamadarin to get them for me and started wearing them day and night. I find some kind of solace in such small acts of rebellion.' I listened silently to Sunita who talked as if the floodgates had finally opened. I realized that not only Sunita, most women here live in 'freedom'.

SUNITA RETURNED FROM her *mulaqaat*.[2] I could see from her face that she was feeling rather low. She beckoned to me, so I went to her. She placed all her bags aside and started to say something, but choked and stopped in her tracks. I silently gave her a glass of water which she took and drank. Tears were streaming down her face and she was wiping them away. I let her recover her composure and then gently asked if everything at home was okay.

She nodded and told me with difficulty, 'My bail has been rejected,' and then started weeping.

This was the second time her bail application had been rejected by the high court. After I consoled her for a while, she brought out the letter that she had smuggled under the noses of the jail security personnel.

Since she and her husband did not get sufficient time at the *mulaqaat*, her husband had written her a letter and slipped it to her. After reading the letter, she told me, 'It seems the judge has placed the condition that bail can be granted only after I spend three years in custody.' We quickly calculated how much more time she had to serve and realized she had six more months before she could be granted bail.

After she recovered her composure, I asked her, 'Why this anxiety to go home? Didn't you say that jail is better than home? And do you know the difference between jail and home?'

She lifted her head in curiosity.

I said, 'Women get beaten for not lighting the stove at home, and here we get beaten if we do.' The women who had gathered around us broke into laughter at this. I continued, 'In Jharkhand, there are power cuts all the time. At home, if there is a power cut, we have to suffer in the heat, whereas in jail, if there is a power cut, they start the generator. Do we have such luxuries at home?'

'If I did not have children I wouldn't have worried so much, Didi,' explained Sunita. 'When I think of them I do not feel like being here even for a moment.'

'I know, Sunita. Who wants to live in confinement even if they are provided luxuries?' I said.

'Very true, Didi, anyone who has been in jail would never want to return again. I went from one jail to another. I will never go back to any jail. I told my husband in no uncertain terms that he should rent a house in Ranchi and only then apply for bail. Even if he doesn't, I am not going back to my in-law's home. I will stay in Ranchi with my children. If he doesn't support me, I will somehow manage my life by giving tuition or by knitting sweaters. I will never go back to that house. I will never attempt suicide like my devrani. I shall live. I shall show the world that I can live by myself. This jail has taught me to have that strength.

'As long as my devrani lived, she was after her husband to separate from the joint family. In our homes, our men do not have backbones. Our men do not have the guts to tell their father that they have a right to take their wives out for shopping. If the elder brother doesn't have the guts, how will the younger brother have the strength to assert himself? My devrani could not adjust to the situation like I did. She felt caged and stifled. She chose her path. I can't understand how she could be so heartless – leaving behind a young child! How could she hang herself? Only God knows.

'I saw her hanging first because her son pulled my pallu, saying, "Badimaa, Badimaa," and took me to their bedroom. I immediately called the other family members. We cut the rope and brought her down from the ceiling fan hoping to save her. But she was already dead by then. This one thoughtless act of hers turned us all into criminals.

'The father-in-law who controls all of us and a spineless husband who could never stand up for me escaped punishment. The only ones who are punished here are me and my innocent children. Do you see how this system of justice works? So unfair!

'Didi, just you watch! From the day I get released, I shall make the decisions about my life. I shall define my own destiny. If my husband joins me, it is fine. If he doesn't want to leave his ancestral home, so be it. I will not worry. I have suffered enough, and my suffering shall end here.' Sunita continued to speak emotionally while I looked on, speechless.

POSTSCRIPT

As expected, Sunita got bail after six months. A few days after her release she sent me a message through the jamadarin. As she had envisioned, she was in Ranchi, and they had rented an apartment where she and her husband lived with their children. She had gone directly from jail to Ranchi. Her husband still seemed to be wondering as to how he would break the news of her release to his father!

– *Translated by* UTLA BALAJI

Ek Chadar Maili Si

NORMALLY, ALL THE WARDS are empty in the evening. Everyone goes out for a breath of fresh air. I was also on my usual evening walk when someone came up and asked me for some medicine for a stomach ache. I went inside to fetch it. The jail authorities had given me a medicine box for emergencies. While I was coming out, I sensed that someone was sitting in a corner. When I looked, I found a woman crying silently, with head bent over her knees. I could make out that she was crying only from the movement of her shoulders. I went closer. It was Sonam. Since I had to give the medicine to the other inmate, I did not stop to speak to her. By then, it was almost time for lock-up, so I could not ask her anything.

Sonam was from Uttar Pradesh. Normally, she would not have caught my attention because she was a very mild-mannered and melancholic person who kept to herself. But when she came to me to ask for my help to draft an application for a *mulaqaat*,[2] the visit from outside visitors, I noticed that she did not speak Jharkhandi. That is how I came to know that she was from Gorakhpur. I remember being a little curious at that time about why she had a case so far away in Hazaribagh but didn't ask her, maybe because I was preoccupied with other things.

After lock-up, I slowly found out the details. Initially, she did not open up. However, after some cajoling, she said, 'Let's go to your place.' We came to my bed. For a while, I asked her only general questions because I was aware that others were trying to listen in on our conversation.

I asked her whether anyone had come to visit her recently. All the inmates are very happy when they have a *mulaqaat* with their dear ones, but soon after, they become depressed. I thought this was the case with her. But she said, 'Who will come to meet me from so far away?' She was right. Travelling a long distance involves a lot of money. Finally, I asked her about her case.

'Who booked a case against you?'

'My brother-in-law's wife belongs to this area. She filed a case against me here.'

'What case?'

'I too don't know exactly. They said it was a dowry case.'

'Did she die?'

'No, no! She is very much alive,' she said hurriedly.

'Then how did they file a dowry case against you?' I asked her in surprise.

'I don't know Didi...'

'Tell me what happened, exactly. I'll find out your case details later. But first, tell me what her allegation against you was.'

She was uneasy, I felt. 'Because he married again...,' she began tentatively, but stopped mid-sentence.

'Who?' I asked. I was very confused.

'He...my brother-in-law.'

'So what if he remarried? What has it got to do with you?'

She hung her head in silence.

Lalita, who had been listening to our conversation from a distance, blurted out, 'Ayyo! Don't you understand anything? Her brother-in-law had a sexual relationship with her.' As soon as she heard this, tears rolled down Sonam's cheeks. She didn't know what to say. Lalita intervened once again and said, 'Don't you know about Sonam's husband's death?'

'How would I know?' I asked, somewhat irritated.

'Didn't you see her name in the register? It is Sonam Mosamath.'

I still couldn't understand what she was saying and asked her, 'So what if it is Mosamath?'

'She calls herself Sonam Devi but actually she is a Mosamath,' explained Lalita. I always thought Mosamath was a surname indicating a caste. Lalita explained patiently, 'Sonam Kumari means that she is an unmarried woman.

Sonam Devi means she is a married woman. Sonam Mosamath means that she is a widow. This is how names are understood here. Don't you understand?'

This made me wonder, why should the names of women be listed like this? In the case of a man, only his caste is listed; if it is a woman, her marital status is indicated in her name. Why do people feel the need to know these things about women?

'Was your brother-in-law a married man when you married him?' I asked Sonam. She nodded in silence. 'Then why should his wife not file a case?' I asked her.

'She never stays with her husband; she is always in her natal home,' Sonam tried to explain.

'But she is still is his wife, she is not divorced,' I persisted.

She simply shook her head to indicate assent. I lost all sympathy for her and said, 'When you involved yourself with a married man with full knowledge, what can anyone do?'

She sensed the lack of sympathy in my tone – it was not like I had tried to hide it – and looked hurt. 'But what can I do, Didi? Nothing is in my hands.' she said.

The misery in her voice irritated me further. How could she say that it was not in her hands? I suppressed a rude reply and said, 'At any rate, you will get bail.' Then I picked up my book to indicate that the conversation was over. She took the hint and went away, disappointed. I was feeling a bit guilty about the way I had behaved but I brushed these feelings aside. Once I began reading my book, I forgot about her completely.

This happened quite some time ago, maybe six months. One day, Doordarshan, the national television channel, showed the film *Ek Chadar Maili Si*. I thought, 'Oh my goodness…I have not even heard that name,' and lay down on my bed. Someone asked me, 'Didi, isn't she Hema Malini?' I put my book aside and looked up. There was Rishi Kapoor in the film too. I did not know they had ever been paired together in a film. My knowledge of Hindi cinema is very poor anyway. I began watching the film. Rishi Kapoor is Hema Malini's brother-in-law in the film. He falls in love with a girl and wants to marry her. Meanwhile, Hema Malini's husband dies. Any woman who loses her husband has to marry her brother-in-law according to the tradition of that place. They are both made to sit at one place and a chadar is placed over them. This is meant to symbolize that from this time, the man has to take care of the woman, whether or not they want to live as man and wife. The wife, in this case, is not allowed or expected to go back to her natal house after the husband dies. This ritual takes place in her mother-in-law's house. The characters played by Rishi Kapoor and Hema Malini are against the marriage but are forced into the new relationship. This is a tradition that has been practised through generations, purportedly to provide protection to the woman once her spouse has passed away. Moreover, it is an arrangement made to keep the deceased son's property in the family. This story takes place in a village in Uttar Pradesh.

I was very disturbed after seeing the film. I got up to go out for some fresh air with a heavy heart. I saw Sonam at a distance. Her eyes were red-rimmed with incessant weeping and she was staring silently into space. A wave of pain shot through me. I nearly collapsed. I remembered the words she had spoken that day, 'Nothing is in my hands, Didi!' Now I understood what she had meant. I silently walked up to her and sat beside her. Shame forced me to remain silent. Only tears can wash away our mistakes so I put my hand on her shoulder and pulled her close to me. Either due to the affectionate touch received after a very long time or due to the pain she saw in my eyes, she hugged me and started crying.

I did not have to say anything. I felt like crying out loudly. The other women present there had tears in their eyes as well, though they didn't know the reason behind our tears. It was a universal grief. I thought, 'How many forms of atrocities are women subjected to! How small is the world that I am familiar with!' I wanted to ask her forgiveness but couldn't open my mouth.

This film was made in 1986. It was based on an Urdu novel written by Rajinder Singh Bedi. I also learnt later that the novel won the Sahitya Akademi Award in 1965. The chadar was an abhorrent tradition that had been practised for a long time in many parts of India. I also came to know later that it was still practised in many places in north India. Though Sonam wasn't exactly covered with a chadar, it was because of this tradition that she had to marry her brother-in-law. Later, when her brother-in-law's wife went to court for her rights, Sonam landed up in jail. As she was imprisoned in a place where people did not know much about this practice, she became a laughing stock among her jail inmates.

Sonam's situation was peculiar. When her brother-in-law's wife filed a case against her, she recorded her name as Sonam Mosamath. Her deceased husband's name was provided as the husband's name. The same continued in her case records too. So she couldn't call herself the wife of her brother-in-law although she was married to him. Since he was alive she couldn't call herself Mosamath either. She faced punishment for no crime of hers. The case was being heard in a place where nobody had an idea about this practice. What could they do even if they knew of it? What has the law to do with it? Whose crime is it? Can the principle of everyone being equal before law bring justice to people in an unequal society? These are complicated questions for which there are no easy answers. This experience was an eye-opener for me. I learnt that nothing is as simple as it looks. One shouldn't jump to conclusions and form opinions in haste, particularly people like me who want to change society. I still feel guilty for judging Sonam without understanding her problem.

Later, she was released on bail.

– *Translated by* Rigobertha Prabhatha

Human vs Animal

TYPICALLY, ALL INMATES cry on their first day in jail, but she had been crying every day since the day she had been admitted here. A soiled sari, a boy in her arms, flies buzzing all around her. There was pathos in her tears. She would not respond to anyone who tried to reach out to her. Some prisoners thought there was maybe a language problem and tried talking to her in different languages. While some prisoners moved away from her in disgust, some others looked at her with pity. Generally, new prisoners were brought to the jail only in the evenings, so it was usually lock-up time soon after they got there.

The pahara (the woman watching over the ward; sentenced prisoners are employed as paharas in jail) admonished her, telling her to wash her hands and feet before the jamadar got there. But she did not respond. She did not even turn her head and look at those talking to her. She was in her own world, crying. After lock-up, she lay down in the place allotted to her, covering her face with her sari. The pahara gave her rotis but she did not take them. The pahara then placed a roti in her child's hand and went away. Nobody talked to her after that.

She sat in the veranda after they opened the lock-up in the morning. She cried intermittently; her eyes had become dry after continuous crying. By the time I completed my morning chores, I received the message that I had to go to court. I saw her as I went to bathe. Due to the flies swarming around her, everybody stood at some distance and looked at her as if she were some strange animal. I went inside and returned with a bar of soap, some detergent and an old dupatta (stole).

When you are arrested, they do not even let you bring the bare minimum necessities with you. People quite literally come to jail with the clothes on their back and nothing else. A new inmate is not even provided soap or oil for their first five days, though this is exactly when you need them the most, since, after their arrest, people would have spent a day or two in police stations, where they cannot take a bath. Hence, by the time they come to jail, they are in a terrible state. I cannot comprehend the rationale behind this inhumane practice.

'Look here, what is your name?' I asked her. She did not even turn her head to look at me. 'Maybe she is dumb,' said someone from the crowd. Realizing that there was no other way to reach out to her, I went and sat next to her. The flies swarmed all around me.

'How long will you cry like this? Get up, wash your face, and bathe,' the pahara said and gave her a neem twig. She continued, 'Look how frightened your boy is.' There was still no movement in her.

'Hey, Didi! It will be all right. Aren't we all there for you?' I said. I held her hand and placed an arm on her shoulder in an attempt to reassure her. It was as if something inside her exploded in response to the human touch. She fell on me and began to weep and wail in a heart-rending manner.

Sakun, who had been standing by and watching till then, came up to us and took the boy in her arms. Then, one by one, the others started coming up to her in an effort to comfort her. Finally, I stood up, pulled her up by the arm, forced the bar of soap into her hand, and sent her to the well. Lalita came up to me and said, 'Didi, we will take care of her. It is time for you to go to court.'

I was no longer needed there. Someone had to take the first step, that was all. After that, everyone began to come forward. By the time I had had my bath, Lalita had bathed the little boy and Sakun had dried him with her towel, powdered him, and applied kohl to his eyes and made a black spot on his forehead to ward off the evil eye. I went to court, relieved. I checked the Hindi newspapers while I was in court waiting to be produced before the judge, but there was no news about her, so I could not find any details of her case.

For some reason, I was haunted by the misery in her eyes.

She seemed like a very poor Adivasi. It was not clear if she was mute or simply unable to speak because she was overcome with grief. When faced with unimaginable difficulties in life, people often go into a state of shock. The situation is much worse for Adivasis living in the forests.

When I came back from court in the evening, I found her in the midst of a group. I thought this was an improvement. She had taken a bath and looked clean. I asked Lalita, 'Did you find out any details? Did she say anything?' Lalita said, 'She is not dumb but we still do not know why they brought her here.'

What we found out later was only the chain of events that happened before her being brought to jail.

One day, she had prepared some gruel, blocked the entrance to her hut with a bamboo partition, and gone into the forest to gather some leafy vegetables. In the meantime, a goat wandered into her hut and tried to drink the gruel. In doing so, its horns got stuck in the vessel. Neither the goat nor the people who spotted it could extract its head out of the vessel. The goat died either due to the gruel choking it or because of suffocation due to lack of air inside the vessel. Enraged, the goat's owners asked her for compensation but she did not have the money to pay them. In the normal course of things, there would have been a village meeting to resolve the issue. But now, police stations have come into the forests, even though other basic facilities are absent. The goat's owners lodged a complaint at the police station. Since she could not pay the compensation, the police foisted some case on her and sent her to jail. Her inability to construct a house that kept out others' dogs and goats had become her crime.

We do not know what difficulties her family members had to endure to arrange for the money, but she finally got bail after three months.

– *Translated by* Surekha Aitabathula

In the Footsteps of Mary Tyler

THERE WAS A HUGE JACKFRUIT TREE in front of the women's ward. They called it the kathal ped. There was a circular, cemented platform under it. We would sit on this and read the papers in the morning. The jamadarin on duty also usually sat there. Three women were given the jamadarin's duty by rotation – two older and one younger. There were always two jamadarins on duty.

One of the jamadarins on duty that day was an elderly woman. She was an Adivasi. This was around the time when I was a new entrant to the jail as a political prisoner. Being from Andhra Pradesh, I had difficulty reading the Hindi newspaper and needed to ask others for help.

The elderly jamadarin came up to me that day and said,

'When I see you, I remember a foreign woman who was here in the past. She too didn't know Hindi and was trying to learn the language, just like you. She too used to deal with the co-prisoners the same way you do now. She too was a political prisoner and was accused in a party case like you. A British woman...'

'Are you referring to Mary Tyler?' I asked eagerly, interrupting her.

She was astonished. 'How do you know about her?' she asked.

'I have read her book.'

The jamadarin was overjoyed. 'Is that so? Do you know, she was a very good person. She wrote about me too in her book.'

I had read Mary Tyler's book in 1992 or 1993 in its Telugu translation. Sixteen or seventeen years later, in 2009, it was rather difficult to recall the details. It hadn't struck me that Mary Tyler had also been imprisoned in the Hazaribagh jail.

The jamadarin continued, 'Amalendu, her husband, was in the men's barracks. Do you know Mr Jha, the warder? He and I were on duty those days. He was two years my senior and was on duty near Amalendu's cell. There was also a Bengali woman – Kalpana. Wards 2 and 3 were used as single cells those days. They kept Mary and Kalpana in separate cells.'

I was dumbfounded. Now, there were thirteen prisoners and four children in each of those small rooms. I went to see the cell once again – the small outhouse in front of the two cells was used by the jamadarins then to keep watch on Mary and Kalpana. When I was in prison it was called the kamanighar and had generally been abandoned by the prison authorities. Convicted prisoners, or kamanis, who were assigned work in return for wages used to cook in that room, and so it had acquired the name kamanighar. This was not exactly full-fledged cooking. It more or less entailed improving on the bland dal given to them either by draining away the water or by adding some onions or tomatoes.

When I knew that Mary Tyler had stayed in that jail, I became restless. I began to feel that I must re-read Mary Tyler's book. I wrote home for the book immediately. Sending letters is a long process. Once a prisoner writes a letter, it must be given to the head warder, who deposits it at the office. Here, it is entered in the register and sent to the head clerk. This man reads it and sends it to the jailor. If it is an ordinary letter, the jailor signs and dispatches it. But if it is written by a political prisoner, then the jailor reads it and forwards it to the superintendent for approval. It is only after the superintendent reads and signs it, that the letter is cleared for dispatch. It takes a week usually to have a letter posted.

So my letter took three weeks to reach home. At that time, my husband was incarcerated in the Hyderabad jail. After my letter reached them, they had once brought him to the Hazaribagh court for a case. He had brought books, clothes, snacks and fruits for me. He obtained the judge's permission to give these articles to me. The judge ordered that the articles be handed over to the police escorting me and inspected thoroughly. The Jharkhand police escorting me inspected the articles in the presence of the AP policemen, court officials and the lawyers of both the parties. However, I was not that concerned about what was there or what was being taken out; I was more focused on the rare opportunity to talk to my husband.

My husband told me that he had got Mary Tyler's book for me. He had only one copy. 'I thought I would ask them to xerox it for you,' he said, 'but then I thought I have brought it all this way – why unnecessarily take it back?'

In the meantime, the police and officials informed the judge that there was nothing objectionable in the articles brought for me. They informed me that they would send them to the jail. However, I did not get my things. After two days, when I enquired after them, I was told that the district police officials had taken them. I had to write innumerable petitions and refuse food to finally get my things. Initially, they only gave me the snacks and clothes. It was only when I began another fast that they gave me the magazines that my husband had brought, but only the mainstream ones. No matter how much I agitated, I did not get Mary Tyler's book and the bag full of other books brought for me. Mary seemed to be giving them tremors even after so many years!

Meanwhile, I came to know that a Hindi translation of Mary Tyler's book was available in the prison library. What an irony! Even though I was not comfortable reading Hindi, I decided to get the translated version. Initially, they told me that the book was out on circulation. I did not get it for months. Finally, the jailor said that he wanted to read it first because he was intrigued since I had been asking for it repeatedly. It took him a long time to finish reading it. He had no time off from duty and could read only bits of it from time to time. I did not give up, and would ask for the book whenever I was taken to court. Unable to bear the constant torment, the jailor finally gave it to me. It took two years from the time I began my efforts for the Hindi book for it to reach me. I also got the Telugu version in my last *mulaqaat*,[2] my last meeting with an outside visitor, before my release.

Mary Tyler was in this jail for exactly five years, from 1970 to 1975. She was taken directly from jail to the airport and sent to London the day the Emergency was declared. They did not allow her to meet Amalendu even once in those five years, not even the day she was deported.

After Mary reached London, she wrote *My Years in an Indian Prison*. It was first translated into Hindi and later into Telugu. I was reading about her experiences in Hazaribagh jail after almost four decades. I was amused to find how little had changed in these four decades, in certain aspects. Chickpeas were given for breakfast even at that time. No one liked to have them for breakfast and would store them for the mahila *mulaqaat* day. This was when women prisoners were allowed to meet their relatives who were in the same jail. Some things had changed, of course. Mary had written that the flies worked the morning shift and the mosquitoes, the evening shift. In my time, the flies and mosquitoes worked both shifts. I used to feel disgusted seeing flies during the night.

They did not allow Mary to meet her partner even once despite his being in the same jail. I was not given permission to meet my husband either, the first time I had requested a *mulaqaat*. I had written to the superintendent immediately, 'The rules say that prisoners can meet their relatives. I too can meet my husband. Why was my right violated? Under what Act did the authorities negate my entitlement? The authorities are obligated to tell me why and I, as a prisoner, have the right to know why.'

The jamadar who had taken my application had told me, '*Mulaqaats* have never been granted to anyone from your party. They will not grant it.'

The superintendent later told me that my petition was discussed by the officials and they knew that there were no written rules to deny my request, and hence, they thought it better to grant it. This was how I was able to meet my husband. Anyway, I had decided to go on hunger strike – the only weapon of protest available to a prisoner – if they did not grant me a *mulaqaat*.

Mary's description of the day of *mulaqaat* seemed familiar. Much like when I was in prison, even during Mary's time the atmosphere would be festive; the women would get decked up as if they were going out to the jatra, the folk carnival, and make pakodas. The only thing that was different was that back then Mary was given rations to cook for herself, and hence was given a stove. So, on the day of the *mulaqaat*, everybody would make some snacks with the chickpeas they had saved, on Mary's stove. Mary would cook only after everyone else was done. When I was in prison, no one was allowed to cook inside the prison. I was told that this was a measure to prevent suicides by self-immolation. Though fire was not allowed inside the prison, we managed to cook something or the other by making small fires with papers, dried leaves or any flammable waste. This was an open secret. The authorities had to look the other way just to keep the agitated women calm.

Once, a young boy apparently brought Mary a flower. She was so moved that she kept the flower in a glass of water. When the superintendent came on a sudden inspection and spotted it, he raised hell, scattering her belongings.

In my time, women prisoners from revolutionary parties are not held in separate cells as the men are. The cells crowded as they were, had been changed into wards. All political prisoners were taken to the courts under heavy security. Often, prisoners could not be taken to court because of a shortage of escort personnel, something that even Mary describes in her book. Handcuffs and ropes were used to tie the hands of prisoners while producing them in the court, though the Supreme Court prohibits this practice. However, women political prisoners were not handcuffed.

In many aspects, though, things had improved. Mary describes how prisoners were not even given permission to wear footwear in the bitter cold. That was not the case in my time. We were allowed footwear in prison. However, we were expected to take off our footwear before entering the jailor's room. I never followed this custom. Once, when a warder told me to leave my footwear outside, I told him that I was not entering a temple, only the jailor's room. That shut him up. Political prisoners were respected by some and feared by others.

Mary describes how she came to prison only with the clothes she had on her person. I was stunned to discover that when she had asked for inner wear, jail officials had written to the Home Ministry. Convicted prisoners were given a uniform. But women convicts were not given any inner wear. They were allowed to get them from home. But most of the convicted women never got any visitors. There was no electricity in the prison described by Mary. We, on the other hand, had difficulty sleeping with the lights glowing all through the night.

Mary saw the reality of life in India in jail. She learnt about the many facets of Indian patriarchy from the experiences of the women who were her fellow inmates. She did not remain silently aghast at the rottenness of the caste system and the practice of untouchability. She proclaimed her opposition to such practices by eating food cooked by a dalit woman who was very friendly with her. Things have not changed much when it comes to the caste system. In a way, the jail upholds the caste system and tries to reproduce the caste-based society that exists outside. Convicted prisoners are assigned work based on their caste. This practice was not the official policy, however, and more a result of the caste biases of the people in charge of assigning work. Dalits and minorities thus face the same fate inside as they do outside. It was only natural then that the Adivasi jamadarin, Levini, had not forgotten Mary. Mary had been very sympathetic to her. She asked me, 'Is Mary Tyler still alive? How can we know for sure?'

Once, during the last days of my prison life, Mr Jha escorted me to the female ward. When I asked him about Amalendu, he fondly reminisced about him, telling me how he was so impressed by that young man that once he had even tried to smuggle a piece of fried fish for him from his lunch box, knowing that Bengalis are fond of fish.

Later, after I had been released, I went back to Hazaribagh jail for a *mulaqaat* with my husband and met old Levini. When I told her what I had learnt of Mary since my release she was overwhelmed with joy.

After my release, I surfed the internet to know more about Mary and learnt that she lives in London. A blog run by a reporter said that he had met Mary in London in 2005. Even though Mary was no longer young, she was still active in combating communalism.

I was able to send Mary a letter through this journalist. I sent my story, 'Oka Paro Katha', which had been translated into English as 'Paro's Children' and published under the same title by the Committee for the Release of Political Prisoners (CRPP). She wrote back to the reporter, 'Your letter brought back memories! Do you know when Anuradha was in Hazaribagh? In any case, it seems to have improved considerably since my time, with milk and fruit for the children, TV, etc.'

A Santhali, Sheela Marandi, who hails from the same

Adivasi community for whom Mary went to Jharkhand and landed up in jail, was influenced by the revolutionary movement. She educated herself in the movement, became a central committee member of the Maoist party, and landed up in the same jail in 2013. She read Mary's biography with fervour. Perhaps that is the logical conclusion for this whole story…or maybe, the continuation!

– *Translated by* Gita Ramaswamy

Lathi Budhiya

'OYE! MADAM!'

The voice rang across the ward like a bell, loud and commanding.

I was taken aback to see it emanate from an old woman whose appearance did not match her voice. Bent with age, she had sunken cheeks, hollowed eyes and partly greying, cropped hair. Her sari was worn above the knees. She had a half-stitched bag beside her that she was working on.

'Come here! Just for a minute!' she called again, waving her stick towards me. This confirmed it; she was definitely calling me.

I thought, 'She could be calling me to thread her needle, but of late, I am having trouble threading needles and am thinking of buying reading glasses…'

'What is the date today?' she asked, interrupting my thoughts.

'The twenty-third of November.'

'How far away is the twenty-sixth of January?' she asked, as if thinking about something.

'Two months.'

'Two months?' she sighed deeply. 'Did you get today's paper? Is there anything about me in the paper?'

What could there possibly be in the papers about her? A little laughter and also a little sympathy rose within me simultaneously. 'Nothing,' I replied.

'These naughty girls are teasing me. If I am not released on the twenty-sixth of January, I will break their legs. Read the English papers carefully as well; news about my release will be published in the papers,' she said.

Then it struck me that 26 January is Republic Day and some prisoners are always released that day for their good behaviour. This was what she was asking about.

'Okay, Chachi. I am also a prisoner like you. But I am like your daughter. So don't call me madam. Call me beti,' I said.

'God bless you, my child! You will go home soon and your husband will kiss you,' she said, pinching my cheeks and displaying a toothless smile.

The naughty girls who were gathered around her laughed loudly, and I was left red-faced.

'This old woman is a rangila – a happy-go-lucky person. She blesses everyone like this,' said Reshmi.

I wondered at the way the old woman threaded the needle with so much ease. She picked up her half-stitched bag and started crooning a song.

This was my first encounter with the old woman. Everyone called her 'Lathi Budhiya (the old woman with a stick)'. No one knew her real name. Some inmates called her 'Chachi'. She always called me 'Madam Beti'. She was reluctant to leave out the 'madam'.

Every morning, after the lock-up was opened, she went to the school verandah near ward no.1 in the women's barracks and sat there with her stitching paraphernalia. She bathed, washed and dried her clothes on the stones under the big neem tree.

Whenever she saw me there, she enquired about Republic Day. The day came and went, disappointing her. After that, she began waiting for 15 August, Independence Day.

SUNDAYS WERE SPECIAL DAYS for the women prisoners. It was the day designated for the *mulaqaat*.[2] They could meet their relatives who were in jail for half an hour after two in the afternoon. Eighty-five per cent of the inmates had relatives in the prison. So *mulaqaat* day felt like a celebration of sorts.

Fire was prohibited in the jail, so was cooking. But on Sundays, some inmates took the liberty of making pakodas for their visitors, using their creativity and imagination. They saved the soaked chickpeas they were given for breakfast every day, dried them in the sun and soaked the dried chickpeas again on Saturday night. On Sunday morning, they ground the legumes on the floor with a stone, and made a batter for pakodas. They picked green peppers from the compound, chopped them and put them in this batter. Three bricks became an oven while sundry things like rags, used saline bottles and dry leaves were burnt as fuel. The mustard oil they were given once a week to use as body oil was saved and used for frying. The aluminium plates provided for eating were used as frying pans.

Some inmates would give one or two pakodas to Budhiya. She would wrap them up in a leaf and carefully tie the parcel to the edge of her sari. Then she would start walking with her cane to the designated place for the *mulaqaat*, singing joyfully. She would always head out for the *mulaqaat* much earlier than the others. Her age did not allow her to walk fast. By the time all the names of the inmates would be called, she would be there to meet her husband and son. The son would talk to her for five minutes, go to the canteen, buy her one or two jalebis and depart. The two old people would be left with each other to share their feelings and their toothless smiles. Their companionship gave joy to all the inmates and jail personnel as well. At a certain point, she demanded that the sepoy let them meet under the tree, which was half way between our wards and the place designated for *mulaqaats*. She complained that she could not hear her husband clearly over the din. When the sepoy said he did not have the authority to sanction this, she chided him, saying, 'Then allow me to go home so that I can talk to him.' The sepoy retorted that he would have gladly sent her away if only he had the power to do so. 'Then send the one who has the power. I will ask him,' replied Budhiya.

A fearless woman, she argued with everyone, including the jail superintendent and the judge. She demanded that they send her home. But they refused, saying it was not in their jurisdiction. People used to say that she was 'barkarar', nobody knew what that meant. I did not understand the word as I did not know Hindi well. Finally, Sunita, the educated one, told me that the old woman, her husband, and her son had all been given life sentences in the lower court. The high court had also upheld it. That is what 'barkarar' means, she said. The lower court's decision would hold as the high court had upheld it. Now, only the Supreme Court had the power to release her.

One day, Budhiya pleaded with me, 'Madam Beti, you have helped many people. If you put in a word for me, I can go home. Please have mercy on this old woman.' I pitied her for her innocence. I was only a political prisoner, not a lawyer. I didn't know anything about law. What could I do except write petitions?

'Your husband is here. Your son is also here. Why do you want to go home?' asked Rinku, who was sitting there.

'Don't I have other children? And granddaughters and grandsons? I wish to see them and spend my last days with them. I don't want to die in this jail. I want to breathe my last at home.' She began to sob. How could I console her?

'Didn't you think of all this when you killed your daughter-in-law?' Rinku asked.

'Did I kill my daughter-in-law? God is witness. He knows everything. He is the one to punish criminals. If I had killed her, God would have broken my head. God will certainly punish the people who jailed me,' the old woman said angrily, pointing towards the sky. Afterwards, she mumbled something in a choked voice, which I could not understand. What I did understand was that she had endured her punishment for a long time. I had no words to describe her agony.

By that time, I had spent three Republic Days and three Independence Days in jail. It was such a pity that she was clinging to life only with the strong desire to die at home among her kin. Later, I came to know about her health issues. She had tuberculosis and her uterus had prolapsed. She had to tie a cloth like a diaper between her legs to push it back. The doctor who would occasionally visit the prisoners, examined her and said that she could not help because the old woman would not be able to withstand surgery at this age. I was shocked to find out how the prolapse had occurred. Right after she had delivered her youngest child, her husband had kicked her in the abdomen during a domestic fight, causing this damage. She badly needed surgery to set it right. But she refused it outright. This was not because there was no money. She refused surgery because she wanted to punish him by letting her uterus hang so that he could never make love to her. This was her rebellion. I was aghast upon learning this.

Was it the height of foolishness or the revenge of a helpless woman? How could she speak so amiably with that man after all the insult and injury he had inflicted on her? How could she crack jokes with him? Laugh with him? I could not understand her. But my affection for her grew with each passing day.

Whenever an officer visited the prison, we would petition for her release, explaining her ordeal. Every officer promised to help her but nothing happened.

Once, after my fourth Republic Day in jail, the old man did not turn up to meet Budhiya on the day of the *mulaqaat*. We soon found out that he had been hospitalized. She was overwhelmed with sorrow. She used to wait for him every Sunday in vain. Meanwhile, her son had been released upon the completion of his jail term.

When the lower court sentenced all three of them, the old people were out on bail for some time, but their son was not. After the high court upheld their sentence of ten years, the old couple was sent to jail again. The son's term had ended because he had stayed in prison continuously. The old couple was yet to complete their term. 'Don't forget me, son!' the old woman sobbed when he was going home.

We received news that the old man was seriously sick and had to be transferred to a hospital. In a few days, she was summoned to the office and taken in a wheelchair, where the old man's body was handed over to his family. Budhiya's grief was boundless.

'Oh mother! Send me home! Let me live until I go home!' she cried, looking up at the sky, addressing her dead mother. Our stomachs churned at this. We were not able to eat a morsel of food that day. I used to sit with her for some time every day, pleading with her or chiding her so that she would eat something. But I had no words to console her.

She asked me to write a petition on her behalf to the jail authorities demanding that they perform the tenth-day rites of the old man and give her a white sari and brass bangles. Her son bought the things needed for the ritual on the ninth day. But she demanded that the jailor provide the things and get the ritual conducted.

I went over to her in the evening. She had bathed, put on the white sari, eaten some food and lain down under the neem tree. She was talking to herself, waving her hands at the sky. 'Look, Madam Beti! See what this old fellow has done! No sooner did I lie down than he came into my dreams, wearing white clothes. You know what he said? He said, "You did everything perfectly, but you could have made some fried potatoes." And then he threw a stone at me. Look at this,' she said, holding up a pebble.

'It could have been a crow,' I said.

'I know his ways. There is not even a single bird on the tree. It is him,' insisted Budhiya. 'The old man must be craving fried potatoes. Please get me some potatoes, I will give you money.' Budhiya tried to untie the knot at the edge of her sari, to give me money.

I refused the money as my eyes filled with tears, blurring my vision.

ONE DAY, SHE SUMMONED ME.

'I want to talk to the jailor. Please ask him to come here,' she said.

'Shall I take you to his office?' I asked

'No, he should come here, he will come if you ask him,' she replied, firmly.

'He won't come if I alone call him, we should all ask him together.' I gathered all the inmates and we decided to boycott all food, from tea in the morning to dinner at night, until the jailor visited us. The jailor grasped the sense of unrest in the charged atmosphere and agreed to come, on the condition that we all ate our breakfast before he arrived. This was his way of establishing his authority. We agreed and he came as he promised. Budhiya stood before the jailor with her cane, her old body bent over in half, her torso almost at right angles with her frail legs. With one hand on her waist, she looked straight into the jailor's eyes.

'Ask him for whatever you want. He will give it,' said Seetha.

The jailor was about to open his mouth to say something but was interrupted by Budhiya.

'Why have you not been jailed yet?' She shot the question at him in a stentorian voice, her face red with rage.

It took a little time for the jailor to understand what she was asking. He was stunned.

'Why were you not arrested when my man died in jail? That is what I want to know,' Budhiya demanded.

'Great! As if I killed him!' retorted the jailor, in a sarcastic tone.

'Then why did you put me in jail? Did I kill my daughter-in-law? You jailed me, my son and my husband because my daughter-in-law died in my house. My husband died here in this jail. So you and your doctor must be put in jail. You jailed all of us, believing my daughter-in-law's people. Nobody believed in our innocence. Now I say that your doctor killed my husband with an injection directed by you. What is your answer? Why are you not in jail on my complaint?' She was holding her stick like a sword, looking at him straight in the eye.

'Hey! Am I not in jail too?' he said in an attempt to lighten the mood as he had no answer to her question.

'You are not in jail. You are in the chair. You should be behind bars, eat what we eat, feel as disturbed as we do – that is what your law says. Why should there be separate laws for us? If it is not so, give my man back to me. If you say that you have no power to bring him back, then send me home.'

The jailor had had enough. 'Send her back to the ward,' he said to the jamadarin.

'What is wrong with her words? You have separate laws for the rich and the poor,' said an inmate.

'What happened to your recommendations for her release?' I was also angry. 'Don't you have the responsibility of writing to the Inspector General about her old age and poor health? Don't you have the responsibility to help her to go to the Supreme Court?' When I said this, every one supported me.

'First, you go and do that, sir,' said Budhiya, waving her stick before the jailor's face.

After this incident, Budhiya's son got a petition written with the help of a lawyer and gave it to his mother along with a letter addressed to me. Budhiya handed them over to me. Her son had written that he would do whatever possible for him to get his mother out of jail and the rest was my duty. I talked to the jailor and made him send the petition to the Supreme Court as a jail appeal.

From that day on, whenever I met her, she would ask me, 'Beti! Have any papers arrived from Delhi?'

Meanwhile, I was granted bail. My fellow inmates were sad and teary-eyed at the news. I hesitated to tell the old woman that I was leaving. But she laughed happily, patted my head, and said, 'Be happy, Madam Beti. God bless you.'

As my husband was still in jail, I went back the next month to meet him. I reached Hazaribagh by mid-noon. The sepoy at the gate said, 'Had you come in the morning, you would have met Budhiya. She was released and left for home only this morning. She fought even with Yama to die at home, among her people.'

My mother had died of a heart attack soon after I was jailed. My sister had given me one of her saris after I was released. I had brought this sari for Budhiya.

The sari, my mother's memory, remains with me, just like my memories of Budhiya.

– *Translated by* P. Sathyavathi

Munni Badnaam Hui

Her name was not really Munni. But everyone called her Munni. She was known to everyone in the male ward and of course, in the female ward too. Being known doesn't mean that she was acquainted with everyone – just that she caught everyone's eye. Her distinct allure drew the attention of all and sundry. Forever laughing and prancing around, she had that perfect natural figure that fashion models strive to achieve through exercise and diet. Several male prisoners diligently kept a tab on the dates of her visits to the court and waited impatiently near the gate to catch a glimpse of her. I understood this over a period of time.

She caught my eye like everyone else's, soon after I stepped into the Hazaribagh Central Jail of Jharkhand, maybe as early as the second or the third day. She was wearing a figure-hugging salwar kameez, her dupatta fluttering over her shoulders like a boat's sail, her hair open and her slim figure jumping, or rather, prancing in the enclosure behind ours. Twenty years old. No, add a year or two. Dusky complexion. Her face glowing with youthful exuberance. An age bereft of all tensions and worries was reflected clearly in her demeanor. She seemed to always be floating half a foot above ground level. She was sometimes heavily made-up. Her nails were well-groomed, long and painted. There was definitely something quite special about her. This was more evident in her behaviour rather than her appearance. She laughed at everything, as we did when we were college students – laughing at and about everything. Why did we laugh? We didn't know! People around us would get quite irritated with our laughter and wondered what made us laugh so much. This girl made me recall my days in college.

'Who is this girl?' I asked the tribal girl next to me.

She answered, 'She's a nachini.'

I was puzzled. What did that mean?

She was surprised that I didn't know the word. 'Nachini means…hmm…' She didn't know how to explain it. Finally, she said, 'You know melas are held regularly here? In such places and elsewhere, dancers dance to the tunes of film songs. They are paid for their performances. She is a dancer – a nachini. Villagers call them nachini.'

'Do such people also get arrested?'

'I don't know! I don't know about her case,' she whispered.

Another inmate who was squatting some distance away got up and ambled to where we were sitting, having guessed that we were talking about that girl. She told us about her without even being asked.

'That girl is here because of a murder. She trapped a rich boy and the boy and she murdered his wife,' she murmured. 'She wears vermillion in her parting, but she is not married...' She had more to say but I stopped her to prevent her from adding more spice to the gossip about the girl. She seemed crestfallen.

At this point, another inmate, Robita, a Bengali woman who had been sent there from the district jail just three days before, walked up to her, eager for more gossip about the girl, saying, 'What? Nachania?' We got up from there and left. It did not escape my notice that after extracting a lot of information about Munni, Robita went to the enclosure behind us and had a long one-on-one conversation with Munni.

Evidently, all the gossip did not bother Munni. She was friendly with everyone. She knew how to administer injections and set up a saline apparatus. Thus, her services were frequently sought in the hospital. She was also called to write letters and petitions for *mulaqaats*[2] and to read the newspaper out loud to those who could not read. She had studied up to the twelfth standard. But her favourite work was that of a beautician. Whenever prisoners went to court or to meet their family members for a *mulaqaat*, they decked themselves up. On such occasions, Munni would cut and style their hair, thread their eyebrows and give them facials. She did this in exchange for a fee and used the money for her minor expenses.

One day, Munni came over and asked me to teach her English. She said that she would come to me every day for an hour in the evening after lock-up. So, every day, she came to my mattress and spent an hour studying with great diligence. Over time, she began to stay back after the lesson to chat for a while. Many people feel the urge to learn English quickly and want to begin using the language as fast as possible. But usually, the excitement to learn wanes within a week. They feel that they have learnt enough. Thereafter, they don't continue to make the effort to learn. It was the same with Munni. But even though her English lessons did not seem to proceed anywhere, she did not stop coming over. I never questioned her about her personal life, though. Nor did she tell me anything.

One day, I asked her, 'Don't you have someone to arrange bail for you?'

'I got my bail long back, Didi,' she replied, 'within six months of my arrest. But the sureties are yet to be furnished.'

'Why is that? Everyone looks forward to bail, isn't it? You said you were arrested almost a year and a half ago?' I was surprised. It seemed quite unbelievable to me.

'His bail was rejected. So I too chose to remain here.'

How incredible! I couldn't refrain from asking, 'Why?'

'We can go out together when he is released.'

I felt that our conversation was going nowhere and

decided to ask her a few straight questions and said, 'Tell me, how was she murdered?'

She burst out laughing, 'Oh! Didi, don't you know? Many stories go around about us in the jail. None of them are true. No one murdered her. She suffered a heart ailment and died of a heart attack. Do think it over. Tell me, is anyone granted bail for murder within six months? That too, in the lower court?' I was not aware of this at that time, but know it for a fact now. In Jharkhand especially, the district court never grants bail in murder cases. One needs to appeal to the high court.

'Then what is your offence? You have been mentioning "him". Who is this "him"?'

'Oh! I will tell you my complete story,' said Munni. Generally, people start their story by giving the name of their village and family. But our Munni was not like everyone else. I knew that Munni was unique, but the way she began her story left me amazed.

'He is my hero.'

Oh my goodness, does this girl live in a dream? I tried to keep a straight face but did not succeed. Munni too started laughing, and said, 'Do you know? I simply adore dancing. I can start swaying to any song I hear. And he is a producer. He produces music video albums and also plays the hero in them. We were a hit pair and he loved me to distraction. There were many other men who fell for me.' There was not a trace of conceit on her face when she said this. She uttered this with great humility.

Private video albums are much in demand these days in Bihar and Jharkhand. These albums are played instead of movies in long-distance buses and on TV channels.

'Since my name was linked with him, men had to be careful about how they behaved with me. But I did have a gruelling time while shooting on sets or on location. You know, people close to him address me as bhabhi,' she said, her eyes twinkling.

'His family is very well off. They are Yadavs. I am from the Ravidas community. That is why his family will never agree to our marriage. Actually, even my family members would not agree. But I have already lost my parents. I have an elder brother; he doesn't do any work, but drinks a lot. I have a younger sister whose education I pay for. The house runs on my earnings. For a couple of years I worked in a nursing home. I was overworked but hardly earned anything. After that, I worked in a beauty clinic and learnt the work, but couldn't put together the money required to start a parlour of my own. If I work for others, I don't earn enough.

'I happened to get an opportunity to work for some albums and a lot of money came in. Moreover, I really enjoyed the work. It's a pleasure to apply makeup. I really love it! As my earnings increased, my brother's drinking also increased. But he disliked me doing this work. I had to hide money here and there to save it from him. Sometimes, when he couldn't locate the money, he would beat me up. He wanted my money but didn't want me to dance. He asked me to stop dancing though dancing was what brought us money – I love to dance.' The happiness on her face as she said that in the middle of relating a gloomy tale conveyed volumes.

She continued, 'Once, my brother really beat me up badly. He used to beat me up often; I used to hide the bruises on my arms and legs with the help of makeup. But that time, my face was swollen. How could we shoot? So I didn't report for shooting. As the crew did not know why I had not come and the shooting was stalled because of me, they were displeased. He made some inquiries. When he located me and saw my face, he asked me to leave my house. "Come," he said, "let's get married secretly. I will arrange a house for us. You can stay there comfortably. Later, we can tell everyone." By this time, people were already talking about us. My brother saw infamy in this, but I saw great support in him. After thinking about it at length, I agreed. We rented a small house to stay in and got married in a temple. We didn't tell anyone about it. Actually my brother feared that he would get no money if I got married. That was his only grouse.'

'Wasn't he already married by then?'

'I didn't find out about that until later. We started a life of our own. He used to return to his home quite late in the night since he had not told his family about us. One day, I pestered him to take me to his house, asking him how long we could conceal our relationship. I thought that I should at least get to know his family. I told him that he needn't tell them that we were married but at the very least they should know that we work together. As he was left with no other option, he took me to his home one day. It was only then that

I came to know that he was married and the father of a small girl. I did not utter a word there, though his family heaped abuses on me. They said that I had trapped him. After we returned home, he fell at my feet. He told me that she had a heart problem and that he was never happy with her. He said that he would die if I was not with him because he was so very happy with me. He began to cry.'

'Don't you think he was fooling you all the while? He kept you in the dark about his marital status. How did you ever believe him?'

She smiled. 'Oh Didi, I was getting beaten up anyway. I thought it wise to choose the pain which came from fewer beatings. I would not achieve anything by leaving him. There are many vultures out there waiting to swoop down on me. As long as I am with him, not even a fly can harm me. I will see what happens once we are released from jail. After that it's my…,' she pointed to her forehead, leaving her sentence incomplete.

'After I visited their house,' she continued, 'his wife began harbouring suspicions about me. They began quarrelling and one day she suffered a massive heart attack. She died on the way to the hospital. Her natal family filed a case against us saying that we had killed her. Initially, his family did not agree to file a bail application for me. But when he refused to sign the *vaqalatnama*,[3] they relented and filed for bail for both of us. I was granted bail, but not him. I decided not to leave the jail without him.'

'You mean that you face a threat from his family?'

'Hmm. If only that were all. But the problem is not simply that. Of course, there is a threat. Actually, right after I was arrested and detained at the station, four men came over to see me. I had a fleeting acquaintance with them. I don't know what they told the SI, or whether they bribed him, but he gave them a chance to speak to me in private for a while. They had a proposal. They said that if I agreed, they would each give one lakh rupees to the police and get me freed directly from the police station.'

She paused here. I wondered about the proposal, but it was not difficult to figure out why the 'kindness' had been shown. Munni laughed and confirmed my suspicions. 'You know what they proposed?' she asked. 'They would rent a flat for me. Every day, one of them would come and spend some time with me. I should have asked them to come together and then they would have ended up stabbing one another.' She burst out laughing at her own joke.

'In fact,' she resumed, 'if I leave jail, they are the biggest threat to me. If they bring along more men like them, what will I do? His family too…it would be no surprise if his elder brother hired goons to kill me or sold me somewhere. So my life is only with him now.'

What a pity, a vibrant girl like her caught in a web of pain and problems! I had not realized but I had said this out loud.

'Oh! You know my problems aren't just outside the jail,' she said. 'They followed me into prison. I had plenty of trouble after I came here. There were four women who tormented me a lot. They talked about me in a very derogatory manner.

They called me a prostitute. They spread rumours that I was arrested because of prostitution and that I was lying that I was caught for murder. They also said that I had murdered his wife by strangling her. They used to abuse me all the time. Once, when I retaliated, they beat me black and blue. I had to defend myself all alone but finally I hit back at them. If I had continued to endure their torment, they would have troubled me even more. Do you know what I did?'

Instead of telling me what she did, however, she began to laugh hysterically. She rolled on the mattress laughing, holding her stomach. She covered her mouth with both hands in an effort to suppress her laughter but broke into loud guffaws and peals of laughter in spite of that. I waited patiently for the mirth to die down, but since it went on for a while, I pretended to be offended. This made her apologize promptly and resume her story. 'The next morning I asked the jamadar (head warder) to get me some paper to write on. When I sat down to write, everyone was intrigued. I addressed the letter to the judge of the district court. The four women were suspicious, but could not ask me about it. They coaxed the jamadarin (female warder) to tell them about it! None of them knew how to read or write. Even the jamadarin was not so good at reading or writing. Nevertheless, she came over to find out. I told her that I was complaining about them and requested her not to tell them.'

'What is so funny about this?' I asked.

'Aha! I don't know how to write a petition to the court! I don't even know if one can plead in that way! I was just pretending to write a petition. The best way to ensure that the jamadarin went back and relayed this to those women was to request her to not do so. I wanted her to go back and tell them. They came to me to offer a compromise as I had expected. After pretending to hesitate for some time, I tore up that paper. And that's it!'

Very impressive!

'What if he is sentenced?' I asked.

'It is quite likely that he will be sentenced. But they may not let things go to that extent. The trial has not yet started, anyway. They will arrive at a compromise with the other party before it does. Actually, all of this would have been taken care of by now. But his family says that they will go ahead with the process only if he agrees to let go of me. He is still in jail because he didn't agree to this condition. Didi! Tell me, once both of us are released, what do you suggest I do? What is the best thing for me to do?'

'What can you do? Your marriage with him is null and void since you have no witnesses. Moreover, his wife was still alive at that time. So the first thing to do once you are released is to insist on a registered marriage. Get married. Make yourself financially stable. Since you have so many skills, choose one among them and make the most of it. Surely, you can't work on these albums for too long. He may look out for a new heroine for the albums once his passion ebbs. As it is, he has cheated on his wife. He is responsible for the death of his wife, whatever you say. You should never forget that. Don't depend on him financially, that's most important.

Start working as a nurse or open a beauty parlour – do some work. If something goes wrong, you will not face too many problems as long as you are financially independent. Since he has been jailed once, he will think twice before cheating on you once your marriage is registered.'

This made her serious. She clutched my hands and said, 'You are so kind-hearted, Didi.' I saw her eyes moisten for the first time. She was not laughing anymore. I could not understand why there was the hint of tears now. I was surprised and wondered at their source. She tried to speak, but her voice was breaking. She camouflaged it with a nervous cough. All the same, a tiny teardrop escaped from her eye and slithered onto her cheek. She flung her hair back and wiped away that tear. I pretended that I hadn't noticed. I picked up the water bottle, took a sip, and casually passed it to her. She drank some water and chuckled. Then she began talking normally, as if nothing had happened, leaving me wondering about the Munni in front of me now and the Munni from a few minutes ago.

'Do you know Robita?' she asked me.

'The Bengali woman? Yes, I know her.'

She introduced herself to me the day I entered the jail. She was quite irritating. She was educated, jailed in a fraud case and had come to the Central Jail from the district jail after being sentenced. She asked me if I had worked for a bank. She probably read about that in the newspapers. When I said yes, she said she too had worked in a bank. I was surprised and told her that I had heard that she had worked for an NGO. She answered that she had worked for an NGO too. Actually, she was arrested on charges of swindling the funds of the NGO. Later, she could never answer my casual questions about her job in a bank. I was amused initially but later felt quite bad for her, though the airs that she put on seemed quite irritating.

'Aah, fie on her! On Teej (a festival when women pray for the long life of their spouses) she led the ceremony and even tried to drag me into it. Anyway, I didn't give her a chance. Ignore her. Now tell me what did she tell you?'

'I wonder if you noticed that soon after she arrived, she took me to the enclosure at the back and talked to me for a long time. We were barely acquainted then. She enquired about me, but I didn't tell her anything in detail, as I did to you. Do you know what she said? She said, "Why do you want to hang around with him? You are still very young. Your beauty will wither away. Now is the time to earn money. If you agree, I will arrange for your surety. If we get together, we will have the world at our feet. I have some wealthy friends. They want company on their tours. I am sure that you can provide them that! You can earn 50,000 rupees in a day and lead a comfortable, happy life."'

I was eager to know Munni's answer to this and my eagerness showed on my face. Munni noticed this and taking pleasure in my keen interest, deliberately sat back, smiling. I chided her, 'Enough of the suspense, tell me what you said.' I regretted it as soon as I had asked Munni the question. I should have been a little more patient.

But Munni chuckled and said, 'I winked at her, saying, "Why should I leave him? I can manage to do what I want to even if he is around."'

I was flabbergasted. Munni burst out laughing.

'Didi, honestly, this is what I told her. This is the perfect answer for such people. Otherwise, she would have harassed me till I agreed. Now I have peace! Would I have come to jail if I had wanted to do something like that? Would I have stayed for so long? Such people just don't understand such things. Just look at her, she pretends to be a dutiful wife and I am deemed a footloose person.'

I was still reeling. I could never have imagined that Robita would have put forth such a proposal to Munni.

An old woman who was snoring happily on the mattress next to me, suddenly woke up and asked, 'Hey girl, who are you calling footloose?'

'It's me, old woman. I am going to elope with your old man!' said Munni. She then got up, jumped over the mattresses and pirouetted away singing a Bollywood chartbuster, 'Munni badnaam hui, darling tere liye (Munni earned a bad reputation for you, darling).

The old woman's jaw dropped. She placed her fingers on her sunken cheeks and wondered, 'Is she a good girl? Or is she nuts?'

– *Translated by* Ratna Madhavi

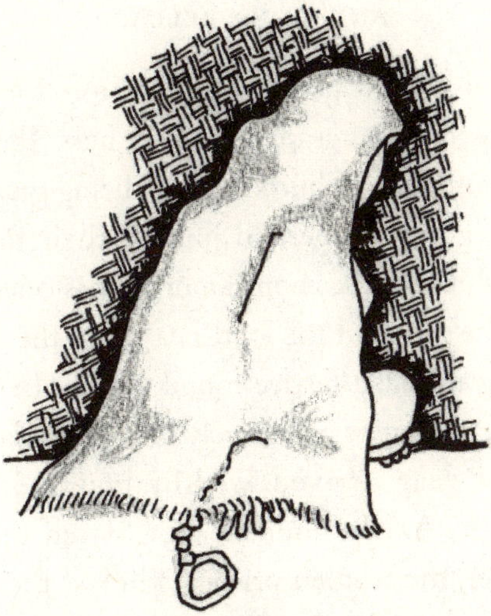

Identity

THE DAY I STARTED TEACHING my fellow inmates the basics of Hindi and English under the tree in the prison compound, I noticed that one of the girls was pregnant. I later learnt that she was already in her seventh month. Her condition distressed me. Delivering a baby is a challenge even when all the facilities are available. Judging by her age, I said to myself, 'This must be her first pregnancy.' And I was right.

Her name was Shilpa. She told me that she knew how to read and write Hindi and wanted me to teach her the English alphabet. She attended the classes every day for an hour or so. Though I had not tried to know more about her initially, very soon, I began to be interested in her. It was the first day of January. Everyone in the jail was excited about the New Year and wondered what it possibly had in store for them. Every New Year raised hopes among the prisoners. They would talk excitedly about the possibilities of bail being granted to them and of their going home and joining their families. New Year's Day, which kindles hope among all, is celebrated in the prison too. The moment the loudspeaker on the central tower starts playing music, a festive mood sets in. In the women's enclosure, the prisoners collectively break into dance.

The new year arrived within two months of my imprisonment. As the loudspeaker blared out one song after the other, the women prisoners linked their hands and danced all through the day. The tribal girls danced without a break, showing no signs of fatigue. Shilpa, who was in the ninth month of her pregnancy by then, joined the dancers for an hour. Seeing her dance with gay abandon made me worry because of her condition. The way she danced surprised me. She was very graceful and never missed a beat. It was then that I learnt that Shilpa, despite her name, was an Adivasi. Besides her name, there was another reason why I had never imagined that she was an Adivasi. Some women prisoners had begun singing bhajans every day and Shilpa would sing along with them. Neither her accent nor her manners had ever led me to think that she could be an Adivasi. It was apparent that she had been exposed to urban culture and as a result, her habits had undergone many changes. However, she had tattoo marks on her forehead, neck and cheeks. This was apparently a common practice among tribal women. I had not paid much attention to these earlier.

When I came to know that she would have to go to the hospital alone, I made some enquiries. I found out that in such cases, the authorities order medical facilities to be made available, but do not grant bail. I was also told that in kidnapping cases, it is very difficult to get bail. In Shilpa's case, I learnt that the appeal for bail had been rejected by the high court. I did not know until then that she was involved in a kidnapping case.

Later that month, she delivered the baby. She went into labour one evening and was taken to the hospital and returned the next day with a baby girl. January is a very cold month in Jharkhand. And yet, the old women in our ward stubbornly insisted on Shilpa being bathed in the veranda before allowing her in, as part of a stupid ritual. Fortunately, the hospital inside the jail had sent a bucket of hot water and some firewood. Apparently, an inmate had once lost her baby in the harsh winter. Since then, the authorities did not want to take chances. When Shilpa returned with her baby, a new life and excitement entered our lives. She named her Chandini; and our entire world revolved around Chandini.

One day, Shilpa asked me to write an application for Chandini's birth certificate. When I had to fill in the father's name, Shilpa mentioned that it was Rahul alias Jamaluddin Khan. That was when I learnt that the father of the baby was a Muslim. I did not press Shilpa for details. The birth certificate did not arrive. After a long wait, I wrote a reminder. The head warder sent for me and explained, 'I know you are trying to help her, but he is not her husband. In fact, they never married. This is why it is taking so long to release the birth certificate.'

I asked him, 'Do you know who my husband is?'

'Of course, I do.'

'How sure are you that he is indeed my husband? You did not witness our marriage nor do you have any evidence.'

'Your case is different,' said the head warder, defensively.

'How is it different? In my case or hers, you will have to go by the husband's name as mentioned in the warrant.'

'It is difficult to talk to you.'

'Then we should not get into these discussions.' I had to tell him to stop him from creating any more fuss over it.

The prison authorities should concern themselves with the behaviour of the inmates and not with what brought them there. It is for the courts to decide whether or not a crime was committed.

Shilpa's conduct was above board in the jail. She never got into any trouble or fights with anyone. She carried herself well and paid a great deal of attention to hygiene and the cleanliness of her surroundings. She came across as a woman of refinement. She never depended on others and at the same time was very caring and helpful towards her fellow inmates. When Chandini was a few months old, Shilpa would carry her tied to her back while she attended to all her work.

One day, a sepoy asked her, 'When you don't have much to do in the jail, why are you carrying the baby around like that? You are suffocating it.'

Shilpa laughed and told him mockingly, 'My dear uncle,

whether in jail or outside, mothers have the same amount of work when it comes to taking care of babies. If you don't understand this, go home and ask my aunt; she will explain to you.' She added, 'In any case, we are used to this. We carry babies that are a few days old – not even months – to the jungle on our backs to collect firewood or to gather mahua flowers. Young Adivasi women do this all the time.'

This surprised the sepoy and he asked her, 'Are you an Adivasi?'

Shilpa smiled and moved on.

When I first heard that Shilpa was arrested in connection with a kidnapping case, I thought she was probably a member of a gang. Many of the inmates had been arrested in such cases. Almost all of them were young Adivasi girls. Once, when we were discussing an incident that occurred in Mumbai, Shilpa intervened and gave us many details. When I asked her how she knew so much about Mumbai, she replied, 'I lived in Mumbai for many years, Didi.'

It was then that she began to narrate her story.

'Ours is a small village in the Giridih district. My parents died when I was very young. Many girls from our village go to Delhi to work. I used to live with my relatives and life was difficult because of poverty. One day, I ran away with some people leaving for work. I was as old as Dalo there,' she said, pointing to the seven-year-old daughter of one of the prisoners.

'What kind of work can a child of that age do? Where did you stay?' I asked.

'I stayed with the girls who I ran away with until they

managed to find work for me. I had to look after children and I was given food and clothes. The employer gave me an allowance as well. I saved money and gave it to my relatives in our village whenever I visited them. As I grew up, I began cleaning dishes in the same household and later, started working as a cook. I was permitted to go home once a year.'

'How did you get involved in the kidnapping case?'

'I later helped many girls from our village to go to the city and find work. On one occasion, when two girls wanted to run away, I helped them. After reaching Delhi, we wanted to inform their parents. When I called my relatives, they told me that the parents of one of the girls had filed a case of kidnapping against me. My relatives wanted all of us to return to the village. As we were packing our bags to leave, the police came and arrested me. Since the case was registered in Hazaribagh, I was brought to this jail.'

'If children leave without informing their parents, the latter would be worried, don't you think?'

'True, but it is a common practice in Jharkhand. When I myself ran away years ago, I found work with the help of another girl. Whether we help them or not, the girls are determined to run away from home. Once they leave home, they face all kinds of difficulties. They often fall into the hands of agents who cheat them or sell them. By helping them, I prevented them from falling into the wrong hands. Yet, they were scared of their parents. Once they returned to the village, one of them told the police that she was drugged and forcibly taken away.'

'Shilpa, even if she had not blamed you for running away, you would have been punished since she was a minor.'

I could sense the fear that lurked briefly in Shilpa's eyes. I immediately regretted what I had said. She was an adult, no doubt, but too young to understand the consequences of her actions.

'When did you get married?' I asked her.

'My employers shifted to Mumbai and took me along with them. Rahul got hired to work as their driver. I used to accompany the children to school in the car every morning and bring them back in the evening. That was when Rahul and I began liking each other and became close. He knew that I was an Adivasi. Since he feared that he might not get a job in Mumbai if his Muslim identity was revealed, he had chosen to call himself Rahul. He was very fond of me and after a while, we got married in a temple. We both continued to work for the same family and shifted to places along with them. Soon after, our employers planned to go abroad on a trip and wanted us to accompany them. Before the passports and visas could be arranged, we thought of going to my village once. I wanted Rahul to meet my relatives. We had a good time in our village. We proceeded to Delhi along with those girls seeking work when we got a call from our village about the case. We were about to leave when we got arrested. After I was brought to the jail, I realized that I was pregnant.'

How complicated Shilpa's life had become! Going by the law, she might have committed a crime. But then, she did it without any knowledge or understanding of the act. My head throbbed. On the other hand, how could one fault the parents who had lodged the complaint against her? They were concerned about their own children, naturally. While seeking a better life, girls like Shilpa willingly take all kinds of risks. In those four years in prison, I saw with my own eyes how young girls like Shilpa aspire to study and obtain a good education.

One day, Shilpa came to talk to me. For the first time, her in-laws had sought a *mulaqaat*[2] with her to see the newborn. By then, she had had her daughter's head shaved in accordance with the Adivasi practice. Her in-laws now wanted her to follow the rituals dictated by their faith, Islam. They gave her clothes and other things and instructed her about the rituals. She showed me those things and began to talk. 'Rahul's parents tried to get him out of jail, leaving me behind. They wanted him to leave me and marry a Muslim woman. This was their condition for arranging bail. Rahul told me, "I will pretend to agree with them and once I am out of here, I will get you out as well." But I was afraid that he might desert me. I took Sunita Didi's advice and petitioned the authorities stating that we were majors and ours was an inter-religious marriage opposed by his parents. I pleaded for legal protection. I then told Rahul about the petition. I made it clear to him that if he got out of jail alone, I would file a case against him. I warned him that this would bring him back to prison. He asked his parents to apply for bail for both of us. They did, but it wasn't granted.'

I could not but admire her presence of mind. 'Is everything sorted out then?' I asked her.

'No. My in-laws now ask for Chandini. They feel that prison is not the right place for a child to grow up in.'

Shilpa told me how she dodged the issue by declaring that her daughter needed to be breastfed. However, now they demanded that Shilpa convert to Islam. Shilpa told me that she had agreed to this. She continued, 'Didi, if I am to consider only Chandini's future, it is certainly better for her to grow up outside prison. But if I send her away, my future becomes uncertain. They may not accept me and they might find another woman for Rahul. Don't you think I am doing the right thing by not sending Chandini with them?'

She needed someone to reassure her and expected this from me. I wholeheartedly supported her decision.

After a few days, I saw Shilpa with her face covered by a dupatta and head lowered. I laughed and asked her, 'What's the matter?' Her dupatta slipped off her head and I cried out in horror when I saw her face. 'What is this?'

'Oh! I did not want you to see me like this.'

Dalo, who was standing next to us, explained, 'She burnt herself with an agarbatti to get rid of the tattoo marks.'

Before I could say anything, Shilpa ran away. From the very next day, she started going to Salima to learn how to offer namaaz.

I FELT VERY SAD FOR Chandini's parents. I came to know later that Shilpa was not her real name. She had changed her name to Shilpa when she had left her village, seeking work. When she met Rahul, she had thought he was a Hindu and started learning bhajans. She did not know then that he was Jamaluddin who had to become Rahul for a livelihood. Both of them had ended up changing their identities. Our society had not been able to assure them that they could pursue better living conditions while keeping their original identities intact. All that Shilpa wanted was to lead a happy family life with Rahul and Chandini. Yes, she still calls him Rahul – the name of the man when she had first met him. For her, he would always remain Rahul.

Soon after Chandini's third birthday, the court announced its verdict. The judge felt that there was enough evidence to establish that the 'kidnapped' girl had left home on her own accord. However, it is a crime to take a minor girl away from her home without informing her parents. Shilpa and Rahul were thus sentenced to four years of imprisonment. By then, they had already spent three-and-half years in prison. Considering their good conduct, a reduction of two months in their jail term was offered and after four months, they were released from prison.

I came to know that Shilpa's in-laws wanted to keep her away from their family until a nikah was performed to formalize the marriage according to their customs. I never heard from Shilpa again. I am not sure whether her dream of leading a happy married life with Rahul and Chandini was ever fulfilled. I hope it was!

– *Translated by* SUDHAKAR UNUDURTI

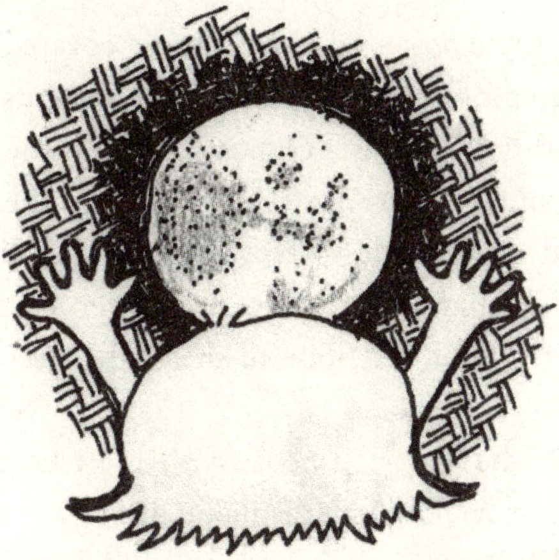

Of the Moonlight that Doesn't Know the Moon

'I learnt something new about my birthday. I was born on Buddha Purnima, according to the lunar calendar, and as you know that is also the birthday of the writer Chalam. Since you have come after so long, I am arranging a small get-together on the day. Some of my close friends want to meet you. Please don't miss this.'

I mulled over the invitation from Swathi. When she called me over the phone to renew the invitation, I accepted.

No one was to be seen when I entered her place. She smiled at me. 'A little surprise for you,' she said, as she took me to the terrace. It had been cleaned. Mattresses covered with bedsheets were spread over mats, with cushions strewn over them. There was a table with some covered dishes and some plates and glasses, indicating arrangements for dinner. There was a dim light in a corner. It was apparent that this was a temporary fixture for this gathering. The mattresses were spread on the side where the light was dimmer. The moonlight felt like a cool mist. As the terrace was on the fourth or fifth floor, the noise of the traffic from the streets was faint.

'I tried my best to get a house with a terrace and coconut trees so that we could watch the moon through the leaves. You have to make do with what you have,' said Swathi. Someone was heard saying, "Where do we get to see coconut trees and leaves amidst a multitude of electric poles?" All of us laughed.

We made our introductions. Some were familiar to me as I had heard their names earlier. Some I didn't know. The ambience was comfortable as there weren't too many people there.

I didn't feel like talking too much in such a romantic setting. However, Swathi proposed that each of us in the party sing a song about the moon or the moonlight.

Pavani asked, 'What about those who can't sing?'

'They can recite the song,' Padma suggested.

Swathi and Madhavi dismissed that at once as an unromantic idea.

Swathi made an alternative suggestion, saying, 'No, in that case, they should narrate a love story. Actually, I had planned that for the second round of activities.'

'Let us start with Madhavi. She sings beautifully,' Pavani

proposed. And it was true. After her song, everyone forgot about the original plan and began requesting Madhavi to sing another song of their choice. She obliged and sang several songs about the moon and the moonlight. Radhika joined her. After that, Karuna sang a few Hindi songs. All of us were in a trance.

Finally, Swathi took over and announced the commencement of the round involving narrating tales of love.

Pavani was the first to rise to the occasion. 'Once,' she said, 'I had to walk a long distance for a story for our channel. It was a moonlit night – just like this one. I wanted to listen to a love story that night and tormented my colleague to tell me a tale of love. It is always easy to talk about others' stories of love.' She then narrated the story she had heard from her colleague.

It was my turn after her. I would have opted to sing a song on another occasion. But not on that night. I said, 'I want to tell a story.'

'Is it another one from the prison?' asked Radhika.

I smiled and remained silent for a moment. Then I said, 'I am not changing our theme. The story I am going to narrate is about moonlight – of a moonlight that didn't see the moon.'

I began, 'You may not find a person who doesn't know of a song on the moon in their language. I qualify my statement with the word "may". Who knows, maybe there is a language that doesn't have a song on the moon. But can we find a child who hasn't seen the moon? This is a question one can answer without any equivocation. No.

'Had I not been to prison as a political prisoner, I would have given the same answer without any hesitation. Often, what we know to be the "absolute truth" is not so. Not that I am unaware of the fact that everything in this universe is relative. I do know that. But I must humbly confess that it was my inability that I could not apply this awareness to everything I knew. So I couldn't imagine children who might not have seen the moon. But there are such children in this world. This is a hard fact that I came to terms with very recently.

'The girl was named Chandini – moonlight. An adorable child, born as a result of the love between an Adivasi mother from Jharkhand and a Muslim father from Mumbai. Both the parents were undertrial prisoners.

'Her mother gave her the name Chandini as she loved the name. Nature is a part and parcel of Adivasi lives. Their names, festivals and daily activities are all associated with nature. When I was in college, a boy received the first prize when he sang a song on moonlight. He sang so well. Do you know how the song went? *Oh moonlight, you shine in a useless place, you shine in a forest*. That was not an age when I could fathom the preposterousness of such an idea. It took a decade for me to realize this. Forests too are inhabited by people; people who are born there. They have made the forest their dwelling place. They do not need electric lamps like us. All their activity is conducted in that faint, cool light of the moon. Even if there aren't any human beings inside the forest, there are many creatures and animals that revel in the moonlight.

Even the trees appear proud, with their green leaves shining in the moonlit night! How can anybody claim a proprietary right over the moon which can both kindle restlessness with its light as well as soothe everyone on the earth? Everyone considers the moon their own. How ridiculous that song was! If only its writer had spent a night in the forest! He would have wept over what he wrote! We can only pity those who say, "Moonlight is wasted in a forest."

'Chandini's mother was a child of the forest who had played in the moonlight. Her search for a livelihood took her to Delhi as a housemaid and that was how she came to see the Taj Mahal in the moonlight on one of her trips with her employer's family to Agra. Before that, she had never heard the tale of Shah Jahan's love for Mumtaz Mahal. When her employers were transferred to Mumbai, she went there with them and it was there that she met Jamaluddin who worked as her employers' driver. My story is not about their love. It was moonlight that stood witness to their love. It started with a life in a moonlit forest in Jharkhand and progressed till they exchanged their vows for a new life before a moonlit Taj Mahal in Agra. They were jailed as a result of trying to help someone. It was only after stepping into prison that she realized that she was pregnant. She named the child Chandini because of its association with moonlight since the child was symbolic of a new light in her life. Thus, the daughter of a woman who had grown up in the forests started her life in a prison.

'Prisoners get locked up before dusk, which is when birds

begin to return to their nests. They get locked up behind the high walls of the stone edifice without ever getting a chance to see the beautiful moon. There are windows in the wards but they cannot see the moon through them. *Chandamama door ki, pua pakayen boor ki* (Uncle moon from afar, makes pua with sugar). Chandini's mother would teach her this song and she would sing it in her cute baby voice.

'We had a television set in our ward in the Hazaribagh Central Jail. However, only Doordarshan programmes are telecast in most prisons. We never missed *Rangoli*, a show playing Hindi film songs that would be telecast on Sundays. The children would be sitting in the front row, watching the programme, their eyes wide open, not even blinking. Children up to the age of five are allowed to stay with their mothers. At any time, the prison had at least twenty to twenty-five children. Dalo was the ring leader of the children. Chandini's mother and Dalo's mother were friends. Thus, Dalo always carried Chandini wherever she went. All the children vied for a chance to carry Chandini. If Dalo deigned to allow someone to do so, the child's heart would swell with joy. Once, Dalo was watching television with Chandini in her lap when a song on the moon started playing. All the children competed to show Chandini the moon on television.

'She had been taught the names of the various objects that she had seen in her surroundings. Whenever she was asked to show an object like the fan, bulb or cat, she would point at the object and smile brightly. But after that day, if anyone asked her where the moon was, she would point at the television. All of us laughed when she did this, including her mother. However, at times, her eyes would well up with tears even as she smiled.

'By the time Chandini reached the age of two, she could identify the moon if she saw it on the television. She would point at it and smile and clap. She had still not seen the moon in the sky.

'That year, on Holi, there was a delay in the preparation of the meal. Holi is celebrated in a big way in Jharkhand, even in prisons. All prisoners are served meat that day. But for some reason, that day, there was a delay and the meat was still not ready by our usual dinner time. What added to the delay was that the meat had to be weighed and portioned into serving sizes of exactly 100 grams for each prisoner before it could be distributed among the inmates. Usually, food distribution was over by 5:30 p.m.; but that day, even at 7:00 p.m. the authorities were struggling to complete it.

'The fallout of all this was that unlike other days, when we would already be in lock-up by dusk, we were all still outside the ward even after nightfall, waiting in a queue for our food. Since it was Holi, it was a full-moon night! Many of us jumped with joy in the moonlight. It was on that full-moon night on Holi that Chandini saw the moon in the sky for the first time. It was a rare occasion – an evening when we were roaming "freely" inside the prison premises; the moon was rising slowly, changing its colour from light orange to a pale yellow. Chandini was the first to spot it! She spotted it before everyone else! From that day, whenever she was asked about the moon, she would roll her eyes and wave her pretty hands towards the sky and say, "It vanished." She never pointed at the television screen again to show the moon.

'Chandini was a fast learner and started speaking very early. She used to repeat whatever was told to her. We would make her talk and laugh heartily. One day, I was preparing some Maggi noodles, having made a rudimentary fire by burning some paper. When Chandini saw me lighting the flame, she ran to her spot and brought her bowl to me. "Please give me some," she said, smiling sweetly. I wanted to tease her and said, "I won't give you anything. Go away." Chandini got cross and replied, "I will fling you away to the moon".

'No one had ever scolded me in such an endearing manner. I was amazed at how the moon had captivated the imagination of such a little soul and smothered Chandini with kisses.'

As everyone listened to the story, standing silently in the moonlight, it was Chandini and her thoughts that shone brighter in everyone's hearts than the moon in the sky.

– *Translated by* SUDHA KIRAN

Paro's Children

RESTLESS AND SLEEPLESS, I tossed and turned in bed. Of course, the 'bed' was just a five-feet long two-feet wide bedspread. Not a double bed that allowed you to turn over at will. If you stretched your legs, you would hit the wall. If you moved an inch upwards, you would bump into somebody. But then, it was not this uncomfortable sleeping arrangement that was the cause of my sleeplessness. It wasn't even the electric bulb that turned night into day inside the ward that was the cause of my unease. Not even the fact that I was in a jail. Indeed, it was not me alone, but all the women in our ward who were facing a similar predicament. The reason behind this – the bloody cats! Yes, cats!

The cats had been a nuisance for a while. We would not

have minded if they only stole our food or drank the milk provided for the children. We would have explored ways to guard both the food and the milk. Winters in Hazaribagh are notoriously cold. The cats would come into the ward quietly, select the most comfortable bed, curl up in the warmth of our feet, and fall asleep. In the early hours of the morning, they would shit on the blanket and run away. The stench of the fresh shit would burst into our nostrils and wake us up. By the time we got up, the cats would have disappeared. The shit would even spill onto the bed at times. Then we would have to throw the entire bedroll out through the grills and wait, shivering in the cold, till the lock-up was opened. This happened every day and somebody or the other would wake up every morning with a scream. Once you have experienced this, there is no way that you can go back to sleep peacefully. You have to spend the entire day washing your bedroll and moving it from one sunny spot to another throughout the day for it to dry. The bedroll comprised a jute mattress stretched on the floor and two folded blankets above it. If you could afford a bedsheet, then you could place one over the bedroll. In winter, we were given two more blankets. They were so heavy that washing them was a big hassle and drying them, even more so.

After going through such an excruciating experience once, people like me started taking up guard duty. On one such hour of hopeless vigilance, I was trying to pass the time by reading a book, when Sakeena told me, 'Didi, you sleep now. Today, the guard duty is mine.' It was the day after Bakr'Id and Sakeena had just had a *mulaqaat*[2] that day. Her visitors had brought some special food for her. She held the packet containing the food in her hands and said, 'Today anyway the billayya (cat) will come to me. Could you hang this packet over there for me?' Sakeena was short. I was possibly the tallest person in that ward. I took the packet from her and hung it on a peg on the wall.

I returned to my blanket and started brooding, staring at the roof. Suddenly, I remembered Paro. 'How nice it would have been if Paro were here now,' I thought, 'These cats would not have been such a menace…'

I shuddered and felt guilty for even having inadvertently sought her presence in prison. Paro had been released after spending not one, not two, but sixteen years in this jail. How unjust of me to want her to be in prison!

I HAD ENTERED THIS PRISON in the darkness of the night. The next morning, Reelamala, who was also a Maoist political prisoner like me, had taken me to ward no. 3 to introduce me to the other political prisoners. There, a crowd had formed around us as we shook hands with the other inmates. They were enthusiastic and asked me many questions. Their language sounded like Hindi but it was actually Khortha and I could not understand it at all. I looked at Reelamala in helpless confusion. She spoke to them on my behalf, giving them all the details they were asking for. Someone brought me two jalebis. I felt embarrassed but thought they might feel offended if I did not take some. I took the jalebis but could not eat them in front of so many inmates. Dividing two jalebis among so many would also be impossible. I placed them in a bowl and put them aside.

Presently, Reelamala said, 'Let us go and bathe.' Sarita and I went along with her to the well. Washing our clothes and bathing took almost an hour. We walked back to ward no. 3, which was Sarita's ward. Since I did not have anything of my own, I had to go to her place. By the time we went there, what we saw was this upturned empty bowl between neatly rolled beds. The lid on the bowl was lying on its side. No jalebis in sight. I was amazed. What was this? Should I expect jail life to be like this? A theft on my very first day!

Reelamala bent to take the bowl and the lid and put them aside. I thought I saw a faint smile on her lips. Or did I imagine it? Sarita, who was behind me, grasped the whole situation in a second and said, 'Surely, this is the work of that badmaash Rudan. Today I will break his legs, just let him come.' She rushed out like a whirlwind in anger and screamed, 'Oye Paro Didi! Come out! Have you seen what your lad has done? While we ignore him, his tantrums increase!'

I was taken aback. A shiver ran down my spine. Why get this angry at a child just for eating some sweet? Why should one raise hell? Would this lead to a big quarrel? I was anxious and followed Sarita out of the ward. In the backyard of the ward there were bathrooms on the left and a well on the right. In between the two was a small dilapidated room. This room was called the kamanighar. A convict doing paid labour is called kamani and the room had got its name from that.

There, in the doorway of the kamanighar, stood a short, dark woman with her hands on her waist. She wore a sari with a flowered pattern down to the ankles and had well-oiled, tightly plaited hair. I thought she was Paro. Several children were playing boisterously in the courtyard. I tried to guess who among them was her son, but failed. I wanted to prevent Sarita from picking a quarrel. I thought I would say, 'Let it be, what can a small child do?' but could not express myself properly in Hindi even in my mind, and remained silent. Reelamala stood there, quite relaxed. The unmistakable smile on her lips, even at this tense time, irritated me.

'Where is your son? Call him!' Sarita said rudely, her face red with anger. I felt perturbed and wished I could vanish into thin air.

But Paro seemed not to care about Sarita or her screams and looked at me with curiosity. 'Is she a new prisoner?' she asked. I smiled affirmatively. She asked me something in Khortha but I could not understand a single word. She spoke with a thick accent. Reelamala replied in Hindi, 'No, she is not from around here. She is from a distant place. She doesn't know Hindi well.' She then told her several things about me. Looking at me in surprise, Paro continued questioning her. I was amazed that Paro did not seem angry that Sarita was making such a hue and cry about her son. 'What kind of a mother is she?' I wondered. Sarita waited impatiently for a break in the conversation. At the first opportunity, she broke in and began taking Paro to task. I picked up courage and politely asked Sarita to let it be. But Sarita simply dismissed my request, saying, 'Why? Why should I let it be? I won't!' She turned her attention back to Paro, and demanded, 'Hey, Paro Di, where is your son?'

Paro looked at Sarita and asked, 'What did he do?'

'He snatched my jalebis and ate them,' said Sarita.

When Paro heard this, she turned her head and shouted, 'Arey o Rudanwaa…aare beta – come, my son.' She called out so loudly that her voice reverberated through all the three wards of the jail. I was startled.

In response to Paro's call, he came skipping from somewhere…and sat down on his hindlegs! He was a cat!

Indeed, a cat.

'See how innocent he looks!' Sarita scolded as Rudan began to meow. I looked at the spectacle in awe. It looked like he was pleading his innocence in his own language. 'Meow…meow…meow…meow – I…don't…know… anything.' I had never seen a cat sitting so obediently and arguing his case.

'Badmaash, if you are hungry shouldn't you have asked me?' Paro asked her son. She then turned to Sarita to scold her, 'Don't you know how to protect your jalebis? Even you cannot hold yourself back when mouth-watering jalebis are placed in front of you. How can he?'

She went in, brought a packet of biscuits and tossed a biscuit towards Rudan. He caught it mid-air, ate it, and continued to meow as if asking for more. This time, even I could understand his language. But Paro did not pay heed to Rudan's pleas and instead called out, 'Arey, Budhan, Sudan, come, come!' The next moment, two more cats appeared. 'Arey langda (lame one),' Paro said, to one of the cats, 'idhar aa re, come here,' as it limped towards her.

The women told me several stories of the pranks the cats played. Jail food was not palatable, even for the cats. Paro used to get biscuits and namkeen made out of maida from the canteen and feed them. Every time a prisoner had a *mulaqaat* and received some food from their visitors, the cats would smell it on them. If the prisoners got something from the canteen, the cats would crowd around them.

It became my daily routine to observe the cats. When the morning tea-bell rang, or when they gave us soaked chickpeas in the name of breakfast, or when our meals were distributed, the cats walked alongside Paro like an escort party. They waited their turn patiently. Their discipline was commendable. They would all fall in line with a single admonition from Paro. Only during winter nights would they come inside the ward to sleep. Paro would make a bed for them by spreading jute mattresses in a corner. They slept like us, covering themselves with a jute sheet.

They were most difficult when fruits and milk were distributed to the children of the inmates. There were about two dozen children with us in the prison. None of Paro's children were in jail. But when milk was distributed to the children, she too would stand in the queue with a bowl. If Paro did not go early to collect the milk, or when she was engaged in some other work, the cats would mew pitiably. Their 'meow, meow' sounded like they were calling out 'maa,

maa'. But they were otherwise very disciplined and waited in the queue patiently along with Paro. How did she inculcate such discipline in the cats?

Initially, the authorities would not allow Paro to collect milk since she did not have any children. But the mothers started complaining that the cats were drinking their children's milk and thus the authorities started giving some milk to Paro for her cats. Of course, this was one version. The other was that it was more out of fear of Paro's tongue than the mothers' pleas that the authorities decided to relent. I soon realized that the second version was nearer the truth. When Paro opened her mouth to yell at somebody, leave alone 'gentlemen', even those who were used to the choicest epithets, would close their ears and run.

But one should concede the truth. No one could find fault with Paro. She never scolded anybody without reason. After the lock-up was opened in the morning, she would finish her ablutions within fifteen minutes and then take up the broom. Tying her pallu tightly around her waist, she would begin her work and not rest till she had finished. Cleaning the entire backyard was her duty. She would clean it well. If, after all that hard work, someone littered or spilt things or sent their children to defecate there, she would then begin – seven generations before them and seven generations after would be blessed with the choicest abuses. If the culprit was unknown then she would scold all the prisoners. In the beginning, I never understood why she was angry and whom she was scolding. I was often irritated. In fact, during the early days, since I did not know Hindi well, most of her scolding did not make sense to me. I heard only sounds. I understood conversations only if I paid attention to each word. When it was a scolding, I would not allow a single word to sink in. I had no interest in Paro, except for her cats.

But soon, I had cause to be concerned about Paro. I entered jail in the October winter. As I was unaware of the severity of the winters there, I was unprepared for the December cold. In the mornings, I would sit in the sun in the backyard with a book or a newspaper. On one of those mornings, Paro was standing there with her hands on her hips, discussing something seriously with five or six other prisoners who were expressing surprise and approval at what she was saying. Rudan ran in front of me, sniffed the soil, and started digging with his forelegs. I had seen dogs do that, but never cats. So, I was interested and watched. Rudan dug a small pit and defecated in it.

Though immersed in the discussion, Paro seemed to have eyes behind her head and shouted, 'Dhak de, beta; cover it, son,' over her shoulder. Rudan faithfully covered the pit with soil, using his forelegs again. How had Paro trained the cats so perfectly? How did the cats know her language so well? I couldn't help but think how well she would have raised her children.

'If you want, let us ask Didi,' I heard Paro say, and came out of my reverie. Since I was a political prisoner and an educated person, all the prisoners, irrespective of age, called me didi. So it was natural that I was a didi even for Paro.

'In yesterday's news, didn't they say something about court?' she asked me. I tried to remember – what had they said about court? Paro, it seems, expected me to say yes. When I could not remember, she looked disappointed. It was then that it struck me. Ward no. 1, where I stayed, was a big dormitory with about seventy people. It was divided into two parts. The separating wall had many openings without doors. One part of this ward had a television which telecast only Doordarshan. Prisoners from the other side would come to this side to watch television. Paro would come punctually in time for the news and sit in the front row. She not only watched the news but also relayed it to the prisoners in the second and third wards. These two wards did not have a television.

Soon after, I came to know something more about Paro. She and her husband had been sentenced for life in a murder case. She had been in this jail for the last fifteen years. She was a very spirited woman.

Within a few days, I understood what had interested Paro. She would watch the English news every day at 8 p.m., attentively. She recognized the Supreme Court if they played a visual of the building. Whenever she heard words like 'prisoner', 'lawyer', 'jail', 'bail', 'judge' and 'punishment', she would immediately come to me to find out more details. She had one recurring question: Had they said anything about the release of prisoners sentenced for life? She would also discuss the news with other prisoners. When a former Chief Minister was arrested and jailed, she gave the other inmates a big lecture on the issue. If she ever saw me around while lecturing others, she would look embarrassed.

Thus, gradually, Paro piqued my interest. I not only started listening to the news attentively but also tried to remember what was said. Every afternoon, she would sit in the kamanighar stitching a ledra (a patchwork quilt) and discussing the news with a group of women. Over time, Paro stopped feeling embarrassed and started inviting me to those afternoon discussions. Starting off with news, our discussions would wander far and wide. But everybody's general concern was discussing their own cases and seeking legal counsel. This way, Paro taught new organizational methods to the organizer inside me. This helped me overcome my language barrier and mingle with all the prisoners. Within a short time, this became a choupal (meeting point) for us.

AFTER SUMMER SET IN, we stopped going out of our wards in the afternoon. On one such afternoon, Paro came to me, her eyes swollen and red. It was clear that she had been crying a lot. I asked her to sit down and tell me what had happened.

'Since last night my daughter has been weighing heavily on my mind, Didi. I am completely broken. Will you please write a pateesan for me?' she asked.

I thought she had mistaken the word 'petition' for something else and asked her, 'Should I write a letter home?' She shook her head, took out an old plastic packet and took out an old, weathered newspaper clipping and a photograph from inside it. The photograph was that of four girls of about fourteen or fifteen years of age. She pointed to one of them, saying, 'She is my daughter,' and handed me the newspaper clipping. The newspaper clipping carried the same picture. 'New Lease of Life with the Help of Missionaries,' said the headline of the story. My eyes skimmed the article. I was dumbfounded and could not say a word.

Paro wiped her tears and said, 'Haan, Didi, my two-year-old child. Her father and I came to jail on a murder case. We were sentenced for life. Where could I have left her? Indeed, there was also another elder girl. I hardened my heart and left her at home. I asked my sister-in-law to look after her. I don't know how she is now, I don't know if she is married…nobody ever comes for a *mulaqaat*. I came to jail with this younger one. They said they allowed children up to the age of five only. But where could I send her after that? Somebody has to come to take her, isn't it? At that time, I was in the Bhagalpur jail. I fell at the feet of the saheb (superintendent) and pleaded with him not to send my child away. She was short, like me, and did not show her age. I would hide her in the backyard during inspections. Thus, she spent twelve years in jail with me.

'One day, the missionaries came. She was fourteen then. There were three other girls – also of the same age – who had grown up in prison. The missionaries said they would educate the children. They said they would provide hostel accommodation for the girls. Saheb persuaded us to let the children go with them. He said he would lose his job if they were not sent away. Some reporters had also come with the missionaries. Everybody said that the children would not be harmed; instead, they would receive a good education. They said that the missionaries were very gentle and that we should send our children with them. I wept a lot but what could I do? Law takes its own course, doesn't it? However, I placed one condition – they had to show me my child at least once a year. They said that this could be done. I made them give me their address.'

She paused and fished out a piece of paper with an address written on it. It said 'St Mary's Orphanage' and was followed by an address. The name of a nun was also written on that piece of paper.

'My child was happy. "Mayya, I will study hard," she told me. In fact, the teacher in the jail school used to say that our Munni was a good student. In fact, Munni taught me how to write my name.' Even in her agony, her eyes brightened for a second.

'Did they ever bring her back here?' I asked.

'Haan, Didi. After one year, I sent a letter to that address and they brought my child to me. However, it has been two years since then, but I have not received any information about my child. I am very anxious. I am afraid. Please write a pateesan to saheb requesting him to have my child brought to me.'

I noted down the address and details, told Paro to be confident, and sent her away. However, that night I could not fall asleep for a long time.

This was all so unjust! A girl entering a jail at the age of two and spending twelve years there! An entire life sentence without committing any crime! The women's jail is a jail inside a jail. The girl had spent all her childhood and adolescence here with no exposure to the outside world. I knew that children were allowed to be with their mothers inside jails till they were five years old. Once the children were six years old, if there was no one to take responsibility for them in their own family, they were sent to government hostels or orphanages. However, often the authorities looked the other way and the children stayed in prison for much longer. Keeping these Munnis in jails without sending them to hostels and the outside world for so long! Should I consider it the benevolence of the jail authorities as Paro does or an irresponsible act?

As a person who had not seen the outside world, how would Munni have felt when she stepped out of prison? So many vehicles, roads, buildings and people! How would she, a person who had never got on to a bicycle or a rickshaw or a bus in all her life, have felt when she boarded a bus for the first time?

I recalled what Bano – who had come from Dhanbad as a convict – had said. She came with a six-month-old baby to jail. After two-and-a-half years, she was convicted and transferred to the Central Jail with her then three-year-old daughter, Roshni. All the convicts in the neighbouring districts were sent to the Hazaribagh Central Prison. All through the journey, Roshni had clung to her mother, crying all the while, afraid that the bus would collapse. Today, there are at least television sets in the ward, which act as a window to the outside world, but during the days when Munni was here, her world comprised only cats, rats, cockroaches, pigeons and mynahs – nothing else. Was Munni like a frog that was raised in a well that had to jump into the ocean?

There was no father or mother to hold her hand and give her courage. How would she have dealt with those she met who did not know anything about the troubles she had undergone, the life she had led? If they ridiculed her saying, 'Oh, you don't know even this little thing!' how would that little girl have felt? I could not calm my mind and felt helpless and anxious. That night too, I tossed and turned on my lumpy bed, unable to sleep.

IN THE MEANTIME, Paro and I began the challenging task of finding Munni. I had already written a letter to the nun whose name and address was with Paro. We waited for two weeks, but we heard nothing. Then we sent a petition through the superintendent of the jail. A month passed. There was no response. Then we asked the superintendent to make a phone call to the orphanage. He said he did not have the number. Paro continued to make enquiries with the authorities whenever they came for rounds.

Finally, the district judge visited as did other judges and legal authorities. Paro confronted them. I explained the issue briefly and asked them to suggest what could be done. The district judge suggested that she petition the superintendent of police. We sent that petition immediately.

Three months passed. Meanwhile, Paro continued to raise a hue and cry whenever someone came to visit us. Just as I was thinking of writing another petition, Paro got a call from the jail office. I waited anxiously till she returned.

Paro returned in half an hour using the choicest abuses. She cursed the head clerk, the SP and the missionaries. Listening to her stream of curses I hesitated to cut her short and ask what had happened in the office. I wanted to wait till her anger subsided. Finally, she said, 'Who did they ask before sending the girl? Saalaah! Why did they send her? They say they sent her to Riwan. How could they do that? You tell me.'

I did not understand. 'To Riwan? Where is that?' I asked.

'Deogarh,' she replied.

I still did not understand. I asked the others. After several rounds of questioning, I came to understand that her daughter had been sent to the remand home in Deogarh where juvenile delinquents are housed. I asked Paro why she was abusing the head clerk. Apparently, he had told Paro, 'Your child might have committed some crime and that is why the missionaries filed a case. Now you have to get her out on bail.'

Paro's wrath peaked. She said, 'Saalaa, why did he send my child to Riwan? What crime did she commit?' and proceeded to unleash a deluge of abuses on him. Gradually, her anger turned into agony. She wailed, 'Didi, my daughter cannot do any wrong. She is a wonderful child. She does not rob or commit any crime. Does such injustice exist anywhere else?'

It was already lock-up time and I could not do anything about it then. I consoled Paro and assured her that I would look into it the next day. The next morning, I asked the head warder to enquire into the matter. In turn, he brought a paper from the office and gave it to me. He told me to explain it to Paro Devi. It was an investigation report sent by the inspector of the concerned police station to the jail through the superintendent.

The report stated that the person to be investigated, one Munni Kumari, in so and so case number, under Section 376, came to depose before the magistrate; that the magistrate had enquired about her parents or guardian; and that after learning that her parents were in jail and there were no other guardians, the magistrate had ordered that she be put under government custody and sent to the remand home in Deogarh.

I strongly reprimanded Paro for weeping and filled her in. I told her that the bada babu had unthinkingly told her whatever had come to mind and that there was no case against Munni. In fact, she had complained against somebody and gone to the magistrate to depose. But I could not understand what her complaint was. I would have to find out about Section 376. But several doubts engulfed me as they did Paro. The missionaries had taken her out from prison. So didn't that make them her local guardians? What had happened to them? Why hadn't they kept her with them? Had Paro not trusted them with her child? Shouldn't they take responsibility, at least till she became a major? Oh! How I wished I knew the details! When I was so agitated, one can imagine how much more agitated Paro must have been.

Paro did not neglect the cats even in this nerve-wracking

scenario. She fed them, caressed them, cajoled them and continued her routine tasks. She did not collapse in despair. It seemed to me that she had found her children in these cats.

The next day, I stopped at the jail office on the way to court and asked an attendant staff, 'What crime comes under Section 376?'

He looked at me with surprise before answering, 'Rape case.'

I was shocked.

Paro had protected her child all these years. How would she take this painful revelation? Would I be able to console her? Did I have the strength to do so? How could I instil courage in her? I went to court lost in a whirlwind of thought. Still doubtful, I asked the bench clerk about Section 376 and received the same response.

For the second time in her life, Munni had to go to jail without having committed any crime. Indeed, how could the magistrate have sent her to the remand home even if there were no guardians? What does the Women and Child Welfare Department do? What happens to the hostels run by them? Munni was a victim and now had become a prisoner without being an accused. How unjust it was that she had to spend life in jail without having committed any crime? Without a single case lodged against her? What kind of democratic country was this? The world's biggest democracy!

Sensing my exhaustion when I returned from court, Paro did not approach me. But I knew that she must have been in agony and went to her immediately to fill her in. But Paro said, 'Didi, never mind. First, wash up and refresh yourself. Then, eat your meal and then you can tell me, in your own time. It doesn't matter.' However much I protested, she would not listen to me and sent me out, since it was already time for lock-up. Once we were in lock-up, we could not wash. There was only one toilet inside the ward, and that did not have running water. Seventy inmates used it at night, each one using only a mug of water. So as the night progressed, the stench from the toilet became so strong that it became difficult to eat inside the ward. So we ate our meals in the open ground after food was served, and before lock-up. On days we had to go to court, there was not much time left to wash ourselves and eat before lock-up after returning to the prison. The roads were so dusty that we had to take a bath after returning, which also ate into the little time we had left before lock-up.

But how could I talk to her once in lock-up? There was no possibility of talking to her in private inside the ward with everyone else around. A crowd of curious fellow inmates was bound to form around us. I had to speak to her privately. Otherwise, someone or the other could say something that could embarrass her. As if she had read my mind, she told me that it did not matter if we could not speak until the next day.

I was restless, embarrassed and impatient. Guilt overwhelmed me. Was it right to not update her as soon as possible, now that I had come to know the truth? Or was it right to protect her privacy? I felt as if I was carrying the weight of the world on my mind.

SITTING IN FRONT OF Paro while she was stitching a ledra in the kamanighar, I wondered how to begin telling her what I had rehearsed several times in my head all night, in order to convey the devastating news as sensitively as possible. I finally mustered enough courage and blurted out, 'The police have investigated. There is no case against Munni. She herself had filed a case against somebody…who raped her.'

I had got across the news somehow, but what would Paro do? Would she scream? Would she be shell-shocked? I looked at her with apprehension. Paro's reaction was not what I had expected.

'So my child complained and filed a case. This means that the fellow will be sent to jail, isn't it?' she said.

'Perhaps,' I answered.

'I know. My child is very brave. She did a good thing.' There was great relief on her face.

I was relieved and seconded her, 'Yes, she did a very good thing. She deposed before a magistrate. Since there are no guardians, he sent her to Deogarh.'

Then I saw anger flash across her face and she launched into a rant against the missionaries. 'Sala log! These mission fellows! I believed them and sent my child with them. When she got into trouble, wasn't it their duty to protect her? How could they abandon her like an orphan? Aren't the people who took her away her guardians? Don't they have any responsibility towards her? I will file a case against that nun! Haan, Didi, can't we file a case? Will you write a pateesan?'

'First of all, we will write a letter to Deoghar. We will ask

Munni to give us the complete details. We can think of filing a case only after we have all the details,' I said.

'Alas, that's true, Didi. Forgive my brashness…haan, Didi, write a letter then,' she said. I asked her what I should write. 'You know everything. Please write it yourself,' she said.

That night, I tried hard to write a letter to Munni in Hindi. In the letter, I asked her to be brave and write to us narrating what had happened. I commended her for filing the case. I read the letter out to Paro the next day and she suggested that I should also ask Munni to take care of her health. Paro told me to instruct Munni to inform the authorities and get medical help if she was experiencing any discomfort.

When I got up to leave, she stopped me, saying, 'One moment,' and asked me to add a few more lines – 'Beti, tum meri jaan ho (My child, you are my life). I live only for you. It's enough that you are alive. Nothing else is important. Only if you are alive can you correct everything else. You have to fight. Himmat rakh (have courage).'

Those words gave me a lot of strength. I had not given Paro courage; it was she who was teaching me. Indeed, when Paro met her husband the next day and told him all that had transpired, it was she who had to console him and instil confidence in him. He almost collapsed upon hearing the news. It was Paro who made him see sense.

DAYS PASSED. There was no word from Munni. We didn't even know whether she had received the letter.

One day, we heard that there was a hunger strike being

called across all the jails of Jharkhand, demanding the release of prisoners who had completed their sentences. This news led to a great commotion. Everybody began coming up to me to discuss their own cases and sentences. We discovered that in our women's ward it was Paro alone who had spent fourteen years or more in imprisonment. At once, it was decided that Paro, along with the rest of us, in her support, should go on a hunger strike. We also decided to send word to the male ward through those who were going to court the next day. Then we had to discuss this with prisoners in other wards. It took us almost a day to prepare a petition and collect everyone's signatures or thumb impressions. Ignoring the condition that a hunger strike notice should be served twenty-four hours in advance, we sent the notice stating that the strike would begin with immediate effect. Since all the women prisoners had given notice on behalf of one woman prisoner, we were immediately summoned by the jailor for talks.

When we met him, he asked us to give him a week's time. We asked him what he intended to do in that time. He showed us the lists sitting on his table that he had received. Among them was a recommendation letter from the jail authorities requesting the release of thirty-three men and one woman (naturally, it was Paro) who were eligible for release. I showed Paro her name on the list. Then she said, 'Okay sir, take ten days, if not a week. But on the eleventh day, we will not give you a pateesan. We will straight away begin anshan (hunger strike). Be ready.' The jailor assured us that it would not come to that and sent us back.

The next seven days saw conversations of release everywhere. Every morning a crowd would gather under the jackfruit tree and enquire whether there was anything in the newspaper. After a week, the newspapers published a list of the names of thirty-four prisoners who were to be released. That day, I must have read the list out about a hundred times. Even if someone knew that her name was not there in the list, she would ask again and again for it to be read out and listen attentively. There was a festive mood in the ward.

Normally, even when an undertrial prisoner would be released, all of us would leave all our work and go up to the gate in a procession to see the person off. So, when someone was being released after sixteen long years of imprisonment, the atmosphere was like a real carnival. Paro's friends packed her things for her in half an hour. Many prisoners began bowing before her, touching her feet and seeking her blessings for their own early release. Since prisoners were getting released in big numbers in the backdrop of hunger strikes in various jails, the media covered the event actively. Photographs were taken and farewell speeches delivered by jail authorities. Thus, Paro received a grand farewell, the kind of which I had never seen during my time in jail. She took leave from each and every person individually.

I expected that Paro and her husband would go to Deogarh immediately.

One morning, a couple of days after Paro's departure, I heard the children scream. I ran out to see what had happened. Budhan, aka 'langda', was dead. I was deeply distressed. The children competed with each other to tell me what had happened. It seems Budhan had stopped eating since Paro left. He would not even drink the milk placed in front of him by the children. The children told me that he was always moving around the kamanighar as if he were looking for someone.

This made me think of Paro's biological children. At least they were happy now, I thought. By now, Paro would have been reunited with her elder daughter who she had not seen for so many years. How must she have felt? Would Paro have recognized her child? Paro had last seen her as a child of five years and now she would be twenty-one. Had mother and child recognized each other?

Somehow, the sorrow I felt refused to leave me. Rudan and Sudan cried all night – 'meow, meow' – in the manner of human infants. None of us could sleep.

One morning when I was reading the newspaper, Reelamala brought a Hindi newspaper and showed me a tiny news item in one corner of the page. 'Reaching home after 16 years, Paro Devi, who was released from Central Prison recently, realized that her elder daughter had died within one year of her arrest. There was no limit to Paro Devi's lamentations when she learnt of her child's death after 15 long years.' I could not recover from my shock.

There was no mention of Munni in that article. But I had full confidence in Paro. Paro was an impregnable protection for Munni now. But without Paro's protection, Rudan and

Sudan had fled somewhere, heartbroken. Perhaps they had gone in search for her.

New cats took up residence in our ward once Budhan died and Rudan and Sudan left. There was no Paro to discipline them. These cats were notorious rowdies. Paro had taken our tranquility along with her when she had left the prison. Nevertheless, mothers like Paro should be outside jails as pillars of strength for the Munnis of the world.

– *Translated by* N. Venugopal

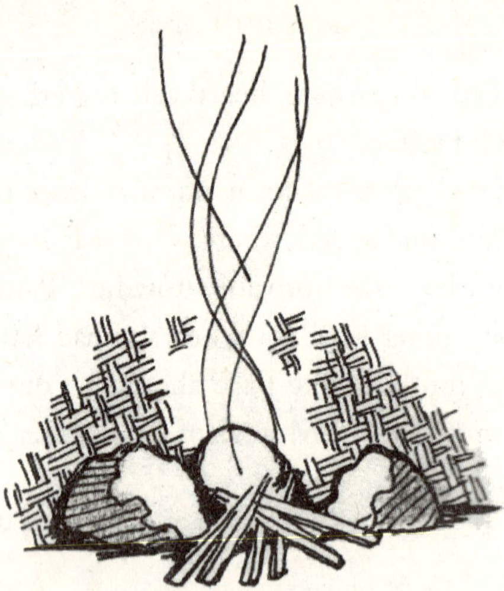

Smoke from a Poor Household

After Sunita was released on bail, the task of entering the names of new inmates into the register fell on me. None of the other inmates was educated. It was an unpaid job as I was an undertrial prisoner, but I agreed to it since it would be a good way to get to know the prisoners as soon as they entered the jail.

Usha and Asha were sisters. Their clothes indicated their poverty but their eyes indicated their knowledge, education and culture. While entering their details, I came to know that Usha was the elder sister. An MA in Political Science, married, twenty-four years old. Asha, MA in Hindi, unmarried, twenty-one years old. They revealed these details with great reluctance. Both of them were weeping copiously so I didn't insist on getting more than the minimum information required. But the other inmates wouldn't keep quiet and kept pestering them, asking, 'What is the case against you? What are you in here for?' To tell the truth, even I was curious. Amidst tears and hiccups, Asha said that it was a murder case. They were not in any condition to say more.

A week passed. The sisters had recovered a degree of composure. Their family came to see them during the weekly visit. That afternoon, I was sitting on my bed, immersed in a Jeffrey Archer novel. To be able to read these kinds of books when in jail is something of a boon. It is an effortless way to pass the time. While I was lost in my book, I thought I heard someone saying softly, 'Excuse me, madam.' I didn't quite understand that it was addressed to me until it was repeated twice or thrice. I looked up and saw Asha, the younger sister, standing at a distance at the doorway of the ward. I couldn't help smiling and indicated that she should come in, saying, 'Is this my private room? Why do you need permission to enter the ward?' She looked somewhat confused. 'Because you are here!' she said. Distracted as I was by the novel, I couldn't understand her, but I said, 'Come in and sit down.' She walked in demurely, her arms folded, and sat down on the floor, a few metres away from my mattress.

'Madam, kindly do us a favour,' she said.

'Arey, why are you sitting on the floor? Come, sit on the mattress. I too am a prisoner like you. Why do you call me madam? Please call me Didi.'

Her eyes widened. 'Oh, really? I shall be back in a minute,' she said and got up again and ran out. She returned soon after with her sister. This time, when I made some space on the mattress, both of them sat down cheerfully, started speaking simultaneously, and then stopped and laughed. 'We thought you were an employee here; my elder sister was scared and pushed me to talk to you,' said Asha, laughing. This was the first time I had seen them laughing in the one week they had been in jail.

'How can you be so naïve?' I asked them. 'If I were employed here, would I have slept here in the middle of all these prisoners?' I suspected that there must be some other reason behind their laughter, but more on that later. They were accused in a murder case and there was no way they could have got bail so soon, but they still seemed to be happy for some reason.

The elder girl ended my confusion by showing me a rolled-up piece of paper that she had been holding in her hand, saying, 'Both of us took a written exam for a job in the DRDA. The results came out today. My younger brother just informed me that I've cleared the exam. My people have informed me that they have called me for an interview. I had come to my parents' house just to write this exam and then got trapped in this case.' The joy in her face ebbed away as she spoke and she started crying.

'When is the interview?' I asked her.

'The day after tomorrow,' she replied.

'Abba! What can we do in such a short time? You have to attend the interview with an escort. For this, you will need the permission of the chief judicial magistrate. You have to write an application and attach the exam result and the interview card. But this is not possible in one day!' I said. A dark cloud passed across her face when I said this. In an effort to encourage her, I said, 'But let's try anyhow. However, we have to wait till tomorrow morning to even meet the jailer.' Her face fell even further at this.

'Who killed whom in the murder you are trapped in?' I asked.

'Actually, there was no murder. They made it up and foisted it on us.'

'How can they file a murder case if no one was killed?'

'An old woman died…' began Asha.

'Let me tell you what happened from the beginning,' interjected Usha. 'We belong to this town. We have our own house. We own a plot of land but because of our straitened circumstances, there is just a tin shed on it. Our father decided that even though we were girls we should be educated, and so he made sure we received a good education. Then he got me married. He spent a lot of money on all of this. Our family doesn't have any inherited property or money. We have always believed that education and culture were our inheritance. Our neighbours are very wealthy people. They try to pick fights with us over every little thing. But we never used to pay much attention. That day, early in the morning, I was cooking in the open compound. That was routine. It was winter and because the wood was damp, there was smoke rising from the fire. My mother was inside the house and Asha and my father were warming themselves by the fire. Suddenly, our neighbours poured water on our fire from the upper storey of their house. And the abuse! The old woman was screaming obscenities. My younger brother shouted back, thinking that keeping quiet would only encourage this behaviour. The man of the house stormed in, caught my brother by the collar and began to beat him up. He pushed my father away when he tried to intervene. My father fell down. Screams and shouts rent the air. We were very frightened. My father fainted. The old woman screamed herself into exhaustion and went in. We felt physically threatened and called the police. It was afternoon by the time a policeman showed up. "Come and file a report," he said and asked us to come to the police station. Just then, we heard wails emerge from the neighbour's house. The policeman went to see what the matter was. Apparently, the old woman had suffered a heart attack. They took her to a hospital immediately. In all that commotion, we didn't get around to going to the police station. But then the sub-inspector came and told us that it may not be safe for us to stay at home. The old woman had apparently died. Saying that we may be threatened by physical harm, he took us all to the police station. There, we narrated all that had happened. He was very sympathetic. The next day he said, "They have filed a case against you and we are helpless." Saying this, they arrested us and our younger brother and sent us to jail.'

'How can this be? Wasn't the old woman taken to the hospital in the presence of the police?' I blurted out. Later, I laughed at my own naïveté.

No matter how many cases one comes across, one is always astonished by some of them. How can people be so horrible and unfeeling? One can only imagine the outcry raised by her in-laws when they found out that their daughter-in-law, who was visiting her natal home, had been sent to prison. Usha also harboured fears on that score.

I told Usha to prepare the petition immediately so that it could be submitted early next morning, as soon as the lock-up was opened. I wrote a petition as well, asking for permission to meet the jailor. I tried to play on his emotions by saying that 'he would be able to lend a helping hand to rehabilitate a life'.

Normally, it is not easy for an inmate to arrange a meeting with the jailor. They refuse permission. But this happened to be a central jail, with judges visiting once a month and other dignitaries dropping in once in a while. This gave us the opportunity to present our issues directly to them. Soon after the jailer had taken charge of our prison, we had also organized a big protest on various prisoners' issues. As a result, he granted me interviews whenever I asked for them. He had learnt through experience that it was better to provide whatever help was possible. He also ensured that he got good press for whatever constructive changes he brought about in the jail. Whatever his reason, I was confident that he would respond positively.

As anticipated, I got a call at eight the next morning. He asked me for all the details. The petition had to go to court and the judge had to agree and grant written permission.

Would it be possible to accomplish this in one day? To add to this complication, Usha didn't have the interview card. The jailer responded positively. He called Usha's home and asked her people to bring the card. He asked us to sit and draft a prisoner's petition. He instructed the head clerk to be present when the court opened, hand the petition to the judge, marking it 'most urgent', stay till the permission was granted, and bring the letter back with him to the jail. It was afternoon by the time the head clerk returned. Then the jailor sent the order to the district superintendent of police, asking for an escort.

The next morning, Usha, escorted by the police, presented herself for the interview. Her family met her there and gave her the certificates. The police escort told the interviewers that it was not appropriate to keep a prisoner outside for too long. So they requested that she be treated as a special case and that her interview be conducted immediately. She was the first candidate to be interviewed. The officials who interviewed her said that the results would be out in fifteen days and she would have to join immediately if she was released by that time. In the event that she was not released, they expressed their helplessness about assuring her the job.

So now Usha had a new cause for anxiety. Would she be able to get bail in time? That a woman prisoner had come to the interview along with a police escort became a big news story for the reporters who had come to cover the event. They went to her house and interviewed people in the neighbourhood, took photographs of the place where they had lit the cooking fire and published a story. As the jailor had hoped, they interviewed him and wrote about how he had helped Usha in the matter.

I advised Usha to keep all the paper clippings of these articles, and in the event of her getting the job, to get her lawyer to file a petition in court, asking for special permission for her to attend work till she got bail. It was clear that a murder had not taken place. Even if they could be held responsible for the old woman getting a heart attack, they could not be accused of murder. Hence, they should be granted bail in the district court. But the district court refused bail for both sisters. However, the high court order for Usha's bail arrived in time for her to join the job. The order came one evening after we were already in the lock-up. Usha's ward was close to the gate of the women's barrack. When they were being taken out, the sisters headed towards our ward to share the news. The head warder scolded them, saying, 'Don't go back in there! There's no time.' Paying no heed to that order, they ran to our ward to share the good news. In those moments of hope and happiness, Usha clasped my hands through the bars and said, 'Didi, you have such a good heart. Please bless me so that my husband will come to take me with him.' Saying this, she bent and touched my feet through the bars, weeping all the while. How nice it would be if only blessings could set things right!

– *Translated by* Sashi Kumar

Where Cooking is a Crime!

THE ENTIRE JAIL PREMISES had been swept clean. There was not a single dry leaf to be found anywhere. How was this possible? It was quite a challenge to keep a household clean with only four or five members. How was it that a jail inhabited by a hundred adults and twenty-five children was squeaky clean? I wondered.

'Didi, they have just rung the bell for breakfast. You sit here. Let me bring it for you,' said Dula. She then ran off with a steel vessel in her hand. I wanted to go and get it myself. Wouldn't it be a nice experience to stand in line and get food along with the others? Since it was my first day, it didn't seem that she would listen to me even if I protested. I let her go. As soon as I saw the breakfast, I was worried.

Earlier that day, I had had the 'prison tea experience'. Before going to jail, I used to think that the 'Worst Tea Award' was reserved for the railways! One sip of the tea served in prison made me change my opinion and immediately give the award to the Jharkhand Central Jail. Oh, my goodness! No one can beat them!

The writer Tripura, in his story 'Bhagavantam Kosam', describes coffee first as 'a hot, wheat-coloured imagination', and then as 'just a wheat-coloured imagination', and finally, as 'just a hot imagination'. But what I got as tea did not fall into any of these categories – it was indeed a strange concoction. Until my release, good tea really remained an imagination, 'just a hot, wheat-coloured imagination'.

Breakfast meant soaked chana daal. Chana daal in any form does not agree with me. Watching my worried face, Lalita asked me, 'Didi, I have some groundnut. Will you have some?' She brought some roasted groundnut and we started chatting as we shelled them. When I was about to get up to throw away the groundnut shells, she said, 'Give them to me.' 'It's okay', I said and got up to toss them away. However, this made Lalita let out a loud scream, as if something terrible had happened. 'Oh, my goodness,' she screamed, 'These are precious! We cannot afford to throw away any of these!' I was bewildered. She looked at me as if she was about to show me a suspense thriller movie. Then she slowly took out three small tins. She set them into a triangle and put a small vessel on top of them. She placed a small earthen lamp under the vessel and added a little mustard oil. Then she took out a small shred of cloth, twisted it like a wick, dipped it into the oil, lit it, and started making what they call 'laal chai', or a tea decoction, in Jharkhand.

'Arey, where did you get this lamp from?' I asked

'We get a lamp every Diwali! It has to be lit somewhere, right? For us, it is lit to make tea. Because it is just tea, this much oil is enough. If it is something more elaborate, then we use groundnut shells, banana peels, old footwear, old clothes, plastic bags, neem twigs, dry leaves…' Her list was not done. It suddenly struck me like lightning why the environment was so spick and span! I witnessed later what kind of wars would be fought over dry leaves. World wars could take place over the hard-to-come-by saline bottles that could be salvaged from the single-roomed hospital in the prison! They burn well and last longer, and so were in great demand.

Fire and cooking – both were forbidden within the jail premises. Even then, people cook some way or the other. Since one cannot cook without fire, all discarded items ultimately found their way to the stove – since there-is-nothing-unfit-to-be-burnt. It was not that everyone cooked, though. Some would bring curries from the men's wards. Convicted male prisoners were given rations instead of cooked food from the jail. They would then cook using these rations and send curries to their relatives in the women's wards. Undertrial men were not afforded this benefit. All inmates were given 15 ml of mustard oil once a week. They hoarded it to use for cooking. That was another big problem I encountered in Jharkhand – the problem of eating food cooked in mustard oil. But this was the only oil they used since mustard is grown here. They also applied mustard oil on their bodies. That was why they were given oil. The prisoners were also given coconut oil once every fifteen days to use for their hair.

For four months in a year, the jail inmates were to be given non-vegetarian food once a week. In case a feast was to be prepared on festivals, the rations given to the inmates could be cut back for two weeks prior to the festival, so that the money saved could be used for the special feast. This rule led to the practice of 'ration cutting' in the jails. If the jailers are to give feasts on festivals, they have to cut rations two months before the festivals. In other words, the prisoners barely received any non-vegetarian food. So, they went after pigeons.

Rinku was an expert pigeon catcher. The jail was in an old building, belonging to the British era. Apart from the high walls and ceiling, there are also pigeon holes in the roofs. Pigeons would keep going in and out of these holes. Some built nests in them. Every morning, the pigeons would look forward to the jail ritual of the drying of the chana daal. They would come in droves for this. One of my friends sent me a book by Dhan Gopal Mukerji called *Gay-Neck: The Story of a Pigeon*. After reading this book, I developed a special fondness for pigeons. In fact, I feel there is a special relationship between jails and pigeons. When they are outside, they seem like symbols of freedom but in jails, they seem like symbols of the loss of freedom. After making it a habit of observing them, I began to notice, for the first time in my life, how beautiful they are – the different types of pigeons, the colours on their necks, etc. Before that, just as all crows looked the same to me, so did the pigeons. At most, I noted that there were white ones and grey ones, that's all. When I saw pigeons, I would often remember Chalam's *Bujji Gaadu*, even though it was about mynas. Once, in a newspaper column by Gopal Krishna Gandhi, I had read about mynas in the writer's balcony. He even seemed to suspect that one female myna was being subjected to domestic violence!

I started reading whatever I could find about birds, and slowly started making birds a part of my life. The jail brought me closer to birds and flowers. They brought beauty and happiness to my life in prison. I am basically a non-vegetarian and am used to eating a variety of meat. However, this newly developed fondness for pigeons placed me in a difficult position and I was called upon to resolve what became 'the pigeon conflict'.

When the pigeons would come by in droves, Rinku would suddenly throw a towel over them. Inevitably, a few would be trapped like this and then she would catch at least one with great skill. On one such occasion, when she was cooking the pigeon, Rudan, the cat, started hovering around her, expecting to be fed. When he realized that she would not give him his share, he enlisted the support of his two brothers, Budhan and Sudhan, who joined him in pestering Rinku. When even that did not work, they sought the help of their 'mother', Paro Devi. All the children backed Rudan and told Paro Devi that they had indeed witnessed Rudan biting the pigeon's neck and killing it. Paro began cursing Rinku – she said that if she treated mute, innocent animals so unjustly, she would get 'bees saal saza (twenty years of imprisonment)'!

Rinku argued that she had not killed, cleaned, marinated and cooked the pigeon just to give it all away to a bunch of stupid cats! But for Paro Devi, they were not 'a bunch of stupid cats' at all. She looked after them as if they were her own children. So there was no question of allowing injustice to be done to them. Paro and Rinku started quarrelling. When two jail inmates quarrel, there is nothing more foolish than trying to mediate between them. But since this was a unique quarrel, with cats (who had the full support of the children) on one side and Rinku on the other, all of us came out of our wards to watch the spectacle that was unfolding. The cats looked like they were ready to pounce on Rinku like a tiger jumps on its prey. To my surprise, it did turn into a big quarrel. Finally, I too was sucked into it and was called upon to deliver the judgment. I decided that two-thirds should be taken by Rinku and one-third should be given to the cats, and that their 'mother' should subdivide that part into three equal parts and feed the three cats. While the quarrel was loud, both Rinku and Paro were shouting at each other partly in jest, which is why I agreed to be the mock adjudicator. Usually, even if a hundred people ask me to intervene, I am not the kind of person who resolves quarrels. Except for becoming an enemy of one of the parties involved, there is nothing more to be achieved.

Rinku glared at Rudan and warned, 'Arey, Rudanwa saala, one day I will cook and eat you too, just watch!'

'Meow,' said Rudan. 'We'll see about that,' it meant. That's what Paro said.

– *Translated by* Gorrepati Samyukta

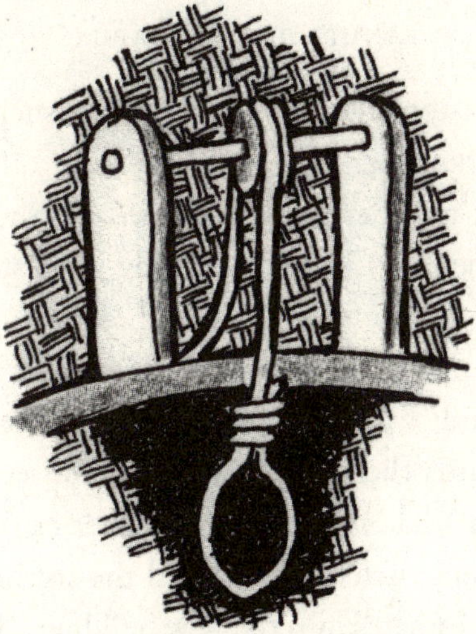

Crime and Punishment

When I first saw her, I thought she was a child going around in a sari for the sake of fun. But such merry-making is usually done with dupattas worn over salwar kameez or with towels. So, not really sure, I peered closer.

There was no doubt that she too was a prisoner. She wore the sari like any other adult. But the enthusiasm and the brightness one normally sees in the eyes of children were nowhere to be seen in hers. I even thought, 'Why ever did they send such a child to the women's ward, instead of the juvenile ward?'

When I greeted her, she became really nervous and scared and so for the rest of that day, I did not ask her anything else. Later, someone told me that she was in prison on a murder charge. I was astonished. How could she, such a little girl, have murdered anyone?

I found out that her name was Shakun. She didn't speak much to anyone, nor did she show any interest in holding a conversation.

I noticed her very late, that is, two years after I had stepped into the prison. It was as though she wasn't there at all. Her ward was towards the rear of the jail premises. Maybe that was one reason I hadn't noticed her. Later on, after the new building was constructed, they closed the smaller rooms and moved half the inmates into the new building. That was when she was moved as well. I was moved into that ward much later. If I hadn't been moved, perhaps I would never have got to know her.

She wouldn't answer any question readily. She was the only one I particularly tried to make friends with. I couldn't believe that she was married. If she had had a frock on instead of the sari, she could have passed for a schoolgirl.

After being told two or three times, she began to show up at the prison school and started to practise the alphabet with the other children. Gradually, she began to make friends. Seeing her laugh and merrily play with the other children, I thought, 'At least she hasn't forgotten how to laugh.'

One day, she came and sat near me. After a while, she began showing me some things in her book that she didn't understand. She had me explain them to her. Then she said, 'Didi! You are a very good person. Whenever I see you, I feel pity.'

I was taken aback for a second. By then I had picked up some Hindi, so I understood what she was saying. I laughed and asked, 'Why?'

'Everyone asks for your advice. Then you'll have to counsel everyone, isn't it? You have to help everyone. I see that and I think, "poor Didi!"'

'At least you take pity on me,' I said.

She must've sensed the amusement in my voice or seen the twinkle in my eyes. She said, 'Oh no! I think I just made a mistake!' and hid her face in her hands, embarrassed.

'No, no, you are right,' I said. 'Anyway, how old are you?'

'I don't know. Guess?'

'Tell me then, how long ago were you married?'

She counted something in her head and said, 'Seven years.'

'How old were you then?'

'Only just this old,' she said, indicating the height she had been with her hands.

'Why only just that old?' I said, imitating her.

'True, Didi. My mother died when I was very little. My uncle and aunt married me off. How long could they nurture me? Once I got married, then the in-laws would have to take care of me, isn't it?' she said, speaking like an adult. Then, feeling shy, she said, 'I wasn't really of age then, but they married me off anyway. It wasn't for several more years that I came of age. Then I was sent off to my in-laws. I was very afraid. He is a lot older than I. You know how old? He has a son older than I, yes!' When she spoke like this, I felt I was speaking to a five-year-old and not at all to a married woman.

'He drinks plenty, used to beat me a lot,' she said, the fear showing in her eyes. 'He used to drink every day; then I had two children.'

My heart sank. This child was so little and already had two children of her own!

'Both the children are girls. That gave him one more reason to beat me up even more. Is it up to me? Can I just wish for a boy and make it happen? One day, he came home dead drunk and began beating me up ruthlessly. I kept thinking of my mother and wept profusely.

I felt like I could not carry on any more. I felt like killing myself. But how could I leave my girls? The elder daughter had just turned three and the younger one was still crawling. What would happen to them?'

As she spoke, I could clearly hear my heart racing, beating faster.

'I took my two little ones and jumped into the well. The water kept pushing me up to the surface. Without really knowing it, I clung to something and hung in there, shouting. Some passersby heard me and pulled me up. I survived but my children died.'

She spoke with her head lowered so I couldn't see the expression on her face. Drawing some lines on the floor with her fingers, she continued, 'I went into shock right there. I didn't go to his house, just sat there. Folks from a house nearby sat with me all night. They called me into their house but I didn't go. They asked all sorts of questions, but I couldn't say anything. Like you, they said, "Poor little girl!" The next day, the police came to arrest me. They said he had filed a murder case against me.'

Seeing the expressionless resignation with which this young child was telling me her story, I came to understand what stomach-churning pain meant.

I cleared my throat and I asked, 'Has anyone from home come to visit you?'

'One time, auntie and uncle came, gave me some clothes, and left. They don't have the money to pay for a lawyer. Didi, that means I can't ever leave this prison, can I?' she asked in a matter-of-fact tone.

'That's not true. When the case is fought and arguments are done, then you can leave,' I said.

'What if I am sentenced?'

'Won't happen.'

I cannot describe in words what a turmoil this girl had caused in my heart.

'Didi! I disturbed you a lot. See, your face has turned pale,' she said.

'Not really,' I said, forcing myself to smile.

I didn't even know what to say or how to behave. After a few moments, she herself got up, saying, 'I will leave you to it; I will come back again later,' and left.

I decided that day that I must get this girl out of prison. I wrote to a few friends who knew the law well. They were in prison as well.

Just as I had expected, soon I received a reply from one of the friends I had written to. 'From what you said, it appears that at the time the case was registered, she must've been a minor. We have to prove this. If she attended any school even for a single year, we should try and obtain a certificate, or we can demand a proper examination by a doctor. But this could be risky. If she was indeed eighteen years or older when this happened, then this could backfire on us. So I think the first option is better. I am also attaching a copy of the Juvenile Justice Act. Take a look.'

When I asked Shakun, she said she had gone to school for a year when she was little, but could not remember either the name of the school or the name of the village it was in. She could not even recall exactly which year it was. Even if she remembered, who was going to get us all those documents!

That put me in a bind. I gathered the details of her case from the prison's office. Next, I petitioned for a government lawyer for her. Once we had a lawyer, we needed to find out if she had been charged or not. But how? Again, I sat Shakun down and started to question her.

She kept responding simply, 'What do I know?' to any question and it was awfully difficult to get the information I really needed.

Finally I asked her, 'Did, at any point, the judge put you in a witness box and ask you "Did you commit this murder?"'

She was quiet for a long while and then said, 'Yes, he did. Not now, but about two years ago.'

This meant that she had spent a whole year in prison before having had any charges framed against her, and that two more years had passed and her case still hadn't progressed.

Perturbed, I asked her, 'So what did you say?'

'I said, "I don't know anything."'

I let out a sigh of relief. This meant that the case would proceed to a trial. I told her that the government lawyer would come and meet her. I instructed her to ask the clerk to let her see the lawyer when she went to the court to sign the papers, but she couldn't muster up the courage to do so.

One more year passed. No progress was made. I tried to help in any way I could, but nothing happened. I even considered placing an official complaint, saying that the appointed government lawyer wasn't doing anything and was no good, but someone warned me that if the judge said anything to the lawyer, the lawyer might taint our case. Seeing that this wouldn't do, I petitioned once again for a lawyer. Then they assigned another lawyer to us.

I waited for one more month and once again wrote a petition to the district judge on behalf of Shakun, stating that there had been no progress in her case in close to four years. I also pointed out that the fact that no enquiries had been made meant that her rights for a speedy trial were being denied.

I wrote this in English and added a note below it: Originally written in English, and translated into Hindi by so and so, and added my name to it and signed. I sent a copy to the district judge. Later, when the district judge came to the prison on one of his rounds, he visited the women's ward. I took a copy of the petition that I had kept with me and stood in the front row with Shakun. If the judge takes just one look at her, it will set right, I thought.

This case was so delicate that it was better for things to move forward rapidly without being bogged down by too many specifics. I was afraid that if I started explaining what had occurred to the judge, then it might amount to an admission of guilt. Oblivious to the thoughts in my head and unaware of such nuances, Shakun kept trying to turn back and run away, out of sheer nervousness. At last I presented her to the judge and told him about the delay in the trial. He was surprised. 'She is just a child!' he exclaimed. 'All right then, you write a petition and send it over.' I had been waiting for just those words. I replied, 'I have already sent it over; here is a copy,' and handed him the petition.

After a few others explained their problems, the judge left, promising me, 'I will surely see to it that this is speeded up.'

Just as he had promised, witnesses were called upon for the next session in court. The lawyer even came up to Shakun and apparently told her, 'You will be going home soon.' An excited Shakun came up to me and told me this.

After three more months, stating that there were no statements against her, and furthermore, that there were no direct witnesses corroborating the allegations against her, Shakun was declared innocent and released.

By then, she had spent five-and-a-half years in prison.

As soon as they began calling witnesses, even her uncle and aunt began to visit the court. The day she was leaving, Shakun's happiness was boundless. She came back from the court in high spirits, saying, 'Didi! I have been released!' and, 'That government lawyer wrote his address on a slip of paper and asked for money. I said loudly, "Where do I have the money?" and then he said, "Please don't shout; if the judge hears you he will scold me".' She kept on laughing. 'Should I bring some money from home and give it to him? Uncle has said he will borrow some.'

'No, you don't need to come to court again and you don't need to pay the lawyer either. The government pays the appointed lawyer a salary.'

Her eyes widened in disbelief. 'You mean I don't ever have to come back? Then can I go home?' she asked.

'Yes, you don't have to be here any more,' I replied. 'Where will you go?'

She became very quiet, and then she said, 'He had come as well. I didn't even look at his face or touch his feet, you know? I asked my uncle, "Will you take me home?" He replied, "That's why we are here!" I then asked, "Would you help me set up a hut next to your house for me? I will work to make my living." He agreed!' She brightened up as she said this and turned to me and said, 'Didi! I can never forget you!'

I drew Shakun closer, hugged her and said, 'Be happy.'

– *Translated by* Raj Karamchedu

TV Serial in Jail – Jail in TV Serial

FREEDOM CAN BE LOST in several contexts. One such context was the inability to escape from television. There are three wards in the women's barracks of the Hazaribagh Central Prison. Initially, only one ward had a TV. After the new building was constructed, all three wards acquired a television. These wards were like social welfare hostels. Each ward comprised a big hall. Everybody sat on their own mattress to watch some TV. Owing to the space crunch, it was not possible for everyone to sit in front of the television set. The volume was, therefore, set high so as to be audible to all. For a long time, I would try to figuratively shut my ears to the sound so I could concentrate on my reading. After a while, however, I couldn't help but join the others who were watching TV. We got only Doordarshan broadcasts, some of which I enjoyed watching. I used to watch *Rangoli* every Sunday without fail. I never gave it a miss because I love old Hindi film songs. Moreover, once I gained some proficiency in Hindi, I even began to enjoy the lyrics.

However, before I went to jail, I never did have the misfortune of having to watch Hindi TV serials. The reason why I began watching these shows regularly was because I saw this as an opportunity to overcome my language problem. When I entered prison, I was not proficient in Hindi. In school, I was one of those who somehow scraped through with the bare minimum marks required to pass the subject. Someone suggested that watching Hindi TV serials would help me learn the language.

The undertrials watched TV with particular interest. If they ever heard words like 'court', 'lawyer', or 'prison', they would ask me to explain what was being discussed or depicted on TV. When they would realize that even I did not really understand the language, they would be quite disappointed. This was also a reason why I began watching some Hindi serials.

Typically, TV serials and films are far removed from reality. Serials or films that depict jail scenes are no exception. As I watched some of them, I could not help but vehemently believe that the directors of these scenes should be jailed for at least six months!

The jail and the police station were always depicted as one and the same, either because our directors do not know that these are two different entities or because they do know but do not care. Upon arrest, a person can be lawfully held in the police station for only 24 hours. Nevertheless, arrested people are often unlawfully held in the police station for as many days as the police wish. And some like me, that is, a political prisoner, come to jail via the CRPF camps or the superintendent's bungalow, bypassing police stations. The police's responsibility in such cases entails producing the prisoners before the court of the magistrate and subsequently handing them over to jail authorities. After that, once trial begins, we generally do not meet the police unless they appear as witnesses.

In movies and TV serials, however, it is a different story. The policeman who makes the arrest is shown seated on a chair behind a table in a hall. On all four sides of the hall are prisoners, behind bars. They seem to be there forever. The policeman talks to them every day. He investigates cases in front of them, listens to those who come to meet the prisoners and solves the cases. In effect, the police station here is the jail. Every serial, at least those broadcast on Doordarshan, almost mandatorily seems to have a jail scene, and this is the manner in which the jail is depicted. With dowry-related harassment, murders and social unrest on the rise, directors know that going to jail has become an accepted reality for many people. It is, therefore, a worrisome fact that they do not pay even an iota of attention to the manner in which jail life is depicted in their work.

Why does it not occur to them that even if the conditions in jails are most deplorable, prisoners still have sheets to sleep on, water pots to drink from and bags to keep clothes in? They show each prisoner in a single cell. So when seventy to eighty prisoners are crammed into one ward, don't you think there will be heartburn? Even when the story is set in a sprawling and busy metropolis like Mumbai, irrespective of the area of crime, the same inspector makes arrests in every corner of the entire city. Although the characters in the story keep ageing, the police and the area remain the same.

There are other strange things. The inspector conducts his daily investigations, issues warnings and beats up the prisoners – all in the jail! Once in jail, the prisoner has absolutely no clue about the progress and direction of the investigation. It is solely the inspector who seems to be privy to this information. In real life, if the inspector wants to seek police custody even to interrogate the prisoner, he has to obtain permission from the magistrate and conduct the enquiry in police stations or unlawful camps. Whoever is arrested is immediately clothed in white in TV serials. In actual prisons, the white uniform is worn only by those who have been sentenced, not by undertrials. In fact, following their arrest, prisoners have to remain in the same set of clothes they were arrested in until their family members arrive with an extra set.

In a particular serial I was watching, the hero's mother gets arrested. In a set which looks neither like a police station nor like a jail, she categorically refuses to eat till her son comes to feed her. Every day, the constable pleads with her to eat and gets really upset when she does not do so. Finally, he approaches the senior officer. The officer locates the son and brings him to her. Only then does she eat. Meanwhile, the constable cannot stop crying. If these gems of directors ever heard the choicest abuses that were heaped on them by the inmates of the barracks as they watched this scene, they would not dare to venture into direction. Or, at the very least, they would definitely refrain from filming jail scenes.

KAMILI WAS NEW TO THE JAIL. She was new to television too. She was a poor tribal woman, who had been leading a nomadic life. For a very long time, she did not know why she had been jailed. Neither did we. Well, that is another story, but for now, suffice it to say that she was very foolish. She quickly earned a reputation for being stubborn and stupid. Her personality soon became a source of entertainment for all the other inmates and a cause for an intolerable headache for the jail authorities.

Rules and regulations were beyond her comprehension. Television was a new-found fancy for her. Added to this, she did not have much to do. The episode in the serial that I described earlier had a most unexpected effect on Kamili. She did not eat the next day, despite pleas from many. Finally, when the head warder arrived, she emphatically said, 'I too will not eat until I see my son.'

'You can see him when he comes for the *mulaqaat*,[2] when he comes to meet you during the regular visit schedule,' said the head warder.

'Go and bring him then,' said she.

When he tried to lock her up, she ran and sat near the

well, saying, 'Didn't the sepoy go and bring Rajvir when his mother refused to eat?'

The female warder standing next to her immediately understood the reference. She had no other job except her duty as a guard, so she too was an avid viewer of television serials. 'Have you lost your mind?' she said. 'Do things like that stuff happen in real life?'

'You think I don't know anything? I saw it with my own eyes,' said Kamili.

The head warder was aghast. He said, 'Who sent you to this jail to torture us?'

This made Kamili angry. She said, 'You khaki-clad fellows, not only do you bring me here, but you dare to question me?'

Following this, it took the jamadar an hour to put her in lock-up.

This 'bring-my-son' drama ran for quite a few days. Eventually, we managed to drill some sense into Kamili and calmed her down.

Some time later came another serial, 'Kasak'. Everyone fell all over themselves to watch it. In this serial, the heroine, Kaveri, is jailed. She is visited by the 'other woman' in her life, Preeti, who not only makes kheer for her and brings it to jail, but also feeds it to her with much love. During our inhumanly conducted *mulaqaats*, none of this is possible. We are unable to even clearly see the face of our visitor because they are a yard away and on the other side of iron grills. We can barely hear each other amidst the din because all prisoners have their visits at the same time. Watching such idealized depictions of *mulaqaats*, which are so far removed from our reality, made us beat our chests in despair.

Every serial was ridiculous. There was an 'other woman' in Kamili's life too. One day, Kamili learnt that the other woman had come to meet her husband, who was also in jail. Naturally, the other woman did not ask for a *mulaqaat* with Kamili. Kamili had a total disconnect with rules and regulations. 'When the other woman in Kaveri's life can come and feed her kheer, why doesn't the same thing happen here?' she thundered. 'You think I am innocent, so you want to take me for a ride? They show almost everything on television, do you know that?' she said to the head warder.

I was reminded of the innocent African hunter-gatherer who was jailed for killing animals for his survival in the movie, *The Gods Must Be Crazy.* Life, as Kamili knew it, is different from the goings on in jail. In her world, reality and rhetoric were not different entities. Everything was as natural as hunger, as real as food. She simply could not understand why events shown on television did not take place in real life. She did not understand the difference between the policeman who arrested her and the policeman stationed in the jail. Film-makers and serial makers are ignorant about the existence of people like Kamili. Nobody has either the time or the inclination to peep into the lives of people like her. We laughed at Kamili's antics, just as we laughed at Chaplin's movies, but no matter how much we laughed, we eventually broke into tears.

– *Translated by* Surekha Aitabathula

The Story Behind the Stories

IT WOULDN'T BE POSSIBLE to write about jail life without having spent time in prison. If one does write about it without experiencing it, it is highly likely that it would be an unrealistic portrayal. However, one also need not think it is necessary to experience jail life before one can use it as a backdrop in one's writing. As for me, I would not have been able to write these stories if I hadn't spent four years in the Hazaribagh Central Jail as a political prisoner.

But that was not my first experience with jail. Two years prior to this, in 2007, I had visited jails in Odisha, accompanying some intellectuals and lawyers. We had visited jails in Bhubaneswar, Berhampur and Malkangiri, on behalf of the Committee Against Violence on Women. We had interviewed jail officials and prisoners as well. However, it was doubtful if the prisoners were able to speak freely in the presence of their warders. It was also obvious from that experience that, as external visitors, the information we can gather about prison conditions is very limited.

However, these stories are not about the prison. It would take a much bigger book to write a comprehensive account of life in Indian prisons. These stories are about the lives of the women prisoners who were my inmates during my time in prison. Getting to know these women and their stories under such circumstances was an educational experience for me. When these stories were compiled and published in Telugu, I was asked how and why I came to be in prison. Readers were curious about me.

My father was the son of a poor, landless, Dalit agricultural labourer. He lost his mother at the age of seven. His father, my grandfather, used to work as an agricultural labourer in the fields of the landlord. One day, while eating lunch in the shade of a tree, he leant back against the tree to rest and never opened his eyes again. Till his last breath, he slaved in the fields of the landlord, but couldn't acquire even a small patch of land. When his son started going 'astray' and caught the education bug, he caned him. Nevertheless, my father joined P.R. College in Kakinada with the money he earned by giving private tuitions. My grandfather died while my father was still in junior college. With great difficulty, my father managed to complete his BA and BEd. My mother is from a lower-middle-class Dalit family. My maternal grandfather did not possess any land, but completed his pre-university course (PUC) and obtained a job. My grandmother studied up to the fifth standard. My mother completed her schooling in a coeducational school, something rare for a Dalit woman in those days.

My parents were greatly influenced by Dr B.R. Ambedkar and dreamt of getting their children highly educated, like him. As a member of the Brahmo Samaj, my father married my mother according to its rituals, without placing any demand for dowry. We are five siblings. My sister is the eldest and I am the youngest, with three brothers between us. According to their principles, my parents waited till they could find a groom who would marry my sister without dowry. They stood by certain values in their personal lives and did not compromise on them. My father died due to a cerebral haemorrhage when I was nine years old. The struggles that my parents had faced collectively now became solely my mother's. She upheld the same values she had while raising us, not taking a single cent in the form of dowry when my three brothers married.

My father worked as a personal assistant to the district educational officer and as a senior schools inspector. But through it all, he never forgot his roots or his origins. Even though he possessed six pairs of suits and six pairs of shoes, he never felt it beneath him to polish his own shoes. He would wear a creaseless, crisp, white shirt tucked into his trousers to his office. He used to put on a coat and travel in a jeep while inspecting the schools, but he always came back home from office on his bicycle. Even though most of the more well-to-do Dalits in the coastal districts were my mother's relatives, when my father died, she derived strength and courage from my father's relatives, who held small jobs or were agricultural labourers. Both my parents, by virtue of their principles and values, made me stand with my feet firmly anchored to the ground.

We were financially in a decent position due to my father's job, but it still did not save me from the insults and discrimination we faced on account of our caste. After our father's death, my eldest brother was attracted by the rationalists, and even though I did not fully understand what it was all about, I was influenced by him and this helped me stay away from religious beliefs and superstitions.

My mother's voracious reading habits were inculcated in me as well. This habit also led to my making good friends, and thereby, being able to access even more good books through these friends. These friendships and books taught me good values and developed a strong conviction in me that men and women should be able to earn their living and stand on their own feet. So I started looking for a job even before completing my undergraduate studies. I got a job in the bank, but even after six years of working and being independent, I couldn't think of getting married. The word 'marriage' was synonymous with a lack of freedom and denoted an irreversible state of being from which there was no turning back. These fears found validation in the dowry-related deaths – murders and suicides – and violence occurring all around me. The strong-willed women character described in some of the progressive literature I had read had made a deep impact on me and I knew that I could never assume the role assigned to women in the patriarchal society we live in, especially the role assigned to a wife. I struggled, wondering if I was the only one with such ideas or if there were others too who shared similar views. I realized that many people were deeply dissatisfied with the current state of affairs, but had resigned themselves to it. I felt that I couldn't do so.

At school, I was always a front bencher. I was awarded the social welfare scholarship, as well as a merit scholarship, which enabled me to complete my intermediate education. I knew that I couldn't afford to pursue professional courses, so I chose B.Com. in the hope it would help me get a job soon. I took the competitive entrance exam for a job in the bank and secured one. I had applied under the reserved category. I took up the job in 1984, while my friends were still studying. We used to discuss reservations. When there were protests against the Mandal Commission for 'merit'-based placements and the scrapping of reservations, I not only remained silent but also suffered from guilt. I used to tell my friends that I would apply under the open category, but they would say, 'There is no doubt you will get a job in the open category. But this means that another reserved person will occupy the seat you vacated. That way you'll make us lose another seat.' And I would cringe with more guilt.

Around the same time, I met Ravi, an RSU (Radical Students Union) activist. When I met him, he had already been arrested, spent a year in jail and just been released. My opinion at the time was that going to jail was akin to one's life and career being destroyed; jailed people cannot lead a 'normal' life in society again. So what prompted him to be willing to risk going to jail even if his life was likely to be destroyed? This curiosity led me to get acquainted with him.

He held alternative views on almost everything. I asked him about reservations and merit on our second meeting. He said, 'Those who propose a merit-based policy do not have clarity of thought. Let's say they are right. Then why doesn't the person who tills the farm own the land? Or, why does a factory worker who participates in production not own a factory?' I was struck by the argument. I began to learn about Marxism and a bigger world opened up for me.

I also did not expect a postgraduate boy from a Brahmin family with a degree in agriculture to express such views. Moreover, Ravi used to do all kinds of household chores that men dislike doing, without making a big deal out of it. I had no idea till then that Marxist politics could change a person to such an extent. It was in May 1990 that I heard from Ravi about an agricultural farmers' and labourers' meeting and decided to attend it. Though everything that happened at that meeting left me stunned, I must talk about one particular incident. The meeting was conducted in Warangal in a large field covered with tents. On the first night of the meeting, there was a sudden bout of wind and rain, which led to a power cut. I did not know anyone there, other than Ravi, who was working as a volunteer. I was alone in the darkness among 30,000 unknown people. It took more than half an hour for the power to be restored. I knew what kind of situations a woman generally faces in such scenarios and was stricken with fright. But I did not feel anyone running their hands over me, even accidentally. I could not believe this because I hadn't known of such a world. At that moment, I very strongly felt that it was worth doing everything we can to work towards such a society. With this kind of awareness, I could not sit on the sidelines any more, simply looking on.

Thus, in 1990, I started my life as a social activist. A year later, Ravi and I became life partners. From 1993, I started working on women's issues. I worked in Hyderabad till 2005, alongside several other women's rights activists. My work not only entailed understanding women's problems, but also building a movement based on these problems and organizing women into collective action. I started working with activists from different economic, cultural and social backgrounds from the undivided state of Andhra Pradesh. By the time I became a leader at the state level, I learnt to let go of many undesirable class traits. I learnt a lot, especially that those who do not develop the patience to listen to others will not become good organizers. I realized that this was the first step towards developing a democratic ethos, that the habit of simply learning to listen needs to be implemented into our lives on a daily basis, like our daily chores. It still stands me in good stead today.

I set foot in Ranchi, the capital city of Jharkhand, on 8 March 2006 for International Women's Day, to organize a seminar on the lives and struggles of Adivasis. By the time I arrived, the participants had already prepared a variety of slogans – 'Jindal, Mittal, Tata ko bhagaao (Get rid of Jindal, Mittal, Tata).' After the seminar, I decided to work alongside the Naari Mukthi Sangh of Bihar and Jharkhand. It turned out to be a great experience. Tribals live in communes so there was no need to tell them to get united. They are already united. During British rule, Adivasis were the first to fight militantly against the British army in various parts of the country. They continue the legacy of resistance to this day.

Despite their deep attachment to the land and their forest-based livelihood, the state is hell-bent on uprooting the Adivasis so it can hand over the valuable metals in the mines in the forests to the corporate capitalists. Jharkhand is known for its rich natural resources and there remains a treasure trove of these resources to be robbed. The Adivasis are fighting for their rights on Jal, Jungle and Jameen. The Santhalihul (uprising), Mundari Ulgulan, was joined by the Hos, Uraons and other tribes during British colonization. Adivasis, who are considered the most backward by the state, are the leaders of the Maoist movement.

Whichever region or field I worked in, the movements I participated in were aimed at transforming the existing society. Unless this happens, it will not be possible to achieve women's emancipation. So I decided very clearly, even in the initial stages of my life as a social activist, that I wanted to be part of such a movement. With this understanding, I became a part of the revolutionary movement in Bihar and

Jharkhand. Ravi had already abandoned his PhD and joined the movement of Bihar in 1997.

We were unarmed when we were arrested in October 2009 from different places in Patna and, after four days of illegal detention, were declared to have been arrested in Jharkhand. In this process, the state violated the law in many ways. That is how we ended up in the Hazaribagh Central Jail. Ravi was moved to Andhra Pradesh within two months. I remained in Hazaribagh for four years. I received a sentence of six months' jail time in a case that ran for four years.

The Hazaribagh Central Jail is a very large jail with 2,500 prisoners. As a woman prisoner, I did not have the opportunity to see all of it. The women's ward is a small jail within the larger jail. It is always kept closed, cordoned off from the rest of the jail.

There were 100–125 women prisoners in the jail. They were free to roam in the yard of the women's ward but at dusk, the ward was locked up. Whenever there was a change of guard, a bell was rung and the shout of 'sab theek hai (all is well)' would echo in the ward, causing prisoners to have many sleepless nights. Being confined within four walls gives rise to a hopeless, dispirited, restless feeling, a sense of suffocation, among the inmates.

There was a space of just 400–500 square yards for us to move around in during the twelve hours a day we were not in lock-up. During the other twelve hours, we were confined to a space five feet long and two feet wide. When life and movement were restricted to such narrow spaces, it was no surprise that the inmates spent so much time shouting, abusing and fighting. When new inmates witnessed such behaviour for the first time, many of them were often stunned. Most people leave jails with a renewed antipathy towards society.

I entered jail as a Maoist political prisoner. It is up to the political prisoner to remember, more than anyone else, that he or she is a political prisoner. Because that helps them remember their responsibility. This is why I tried to understand if the reasons behind the fights in the jail were what they seemed to be on the outside or if there was more to them. This required patience and tolerance. However, sometimes I lost patience and yelled at the women. Even though it did put an end to the fighting, I realized that this was a wrong approach and apologized. The other inmates would feel bad and say, 'You only did it for our sake.' But I told them that I had no right to exert authority over them and that they should question me if I behaved that way. I understood them only because of the principles and values that I tried to follow. It was probably then that other prisoners saw the difference between a regular prisoner and a political prisoner. I was sure that unless one possesses such political insight, it would not be possible to understand these women prisoners. I decided not to be judgmental about anyone. I realized that even though I did not know what kind of people they were, it would be good for me to understand them since I needed to live with them for the foreseeable future (though I did not know then for how long).

I saw women who were extremely superstitious, as well as women like Reelamala, who were inspired and shaped by the revolutionary movement. This contrast became the basis of the first story I wrote while still in jail, titled 'Commerce with the Supernatural!' Then, after seeing Paro's cats, I wrote a letter to political prisoners in the Nagpur jail about her. They suggested that I write my observations down in the form of a story. My initial opinion of Paro gradually underwent a change as I came to know her. Paro had come to prison on a murder charge. I had no idea if she had really murdered anyone and, if she had, what were the circumstances that had led to the murder. I never asked her. They were all women, so it was unlikely for them to have committed brutal murders. There were very few inmates in there who had been charged with that kind of crime. These women were mostly victims of patriarchy. They were perpetrators as much as they were victims.

Shakun, who married at a young age and wanted to die to escape the violence of her husband; Shilpa, who ran away from her home in search of a better life; Durga, who couldn't take caste abuse from a woman any more and attacked her without any intention of killing her; Munni, who considered jail a safe place to be in once the man who deceived her also became the only man who could protect her, all because she could not find a respectable job, or rather, the job she found was not deemed respectable; and Sonam, who was jailed for marrying her brother-in-law, despite not having any say in that marriage – all these women were criminals in the eyes of law. But after listening to their stories, one wondered what constitutes a crime. Who does the law protect? Are the laws of the land capable of rendering justice to people of the most oppressed strata of society, to classes and social groups that are exploited? One wonders if the existing laws are even being implemented fairly.

The stories of these fellow women inmates made one question the relevance of the existing system. Phoolmuni, who was a goatherd in the forest, was in jail as a Maoist prisoner; a helpless Adivasi woman was jailed because a goat's head got stuck in a pot; two sisters were jailed for a fight that resulted from smoke, and arrested on murder charges for a crime they had not committed; young children lost out on their childhood, simply because their mother's 'crime' landed her in jail.

It is not just the women in these stories – all women who are imprisoned have tragic stories to tell. One might ask, 'Don't women commit any crimes?' But what of the society that creates the conditions that lead to such crimes being committed? There is no doubt that there are women who commit heinous crimes. But such women are rarely jailed and even if they are, they don't spend much time in jail. Our legal system is indeed unjust.

I did not write these stories only to talk about life in prison. I did so to bring to light the tragic tales of women who are imprisoned. While doing so, I consciously did not focus only on the horrific difficulties faced by these women. We all love Charlie Chaplin's films; they make us laugh, but they also make us cry. And then they make us think. Hence, I also wrote about situations in jails that make us laugh. When these stories were published individually – and especially when they were serialized in *Andhra Jyothi* for ten weeks – the response was beyond my expectations. I don't believe that it was a response to my stories because these are not stories! The response was an outpouring of support in response to the women in these stories and many more such women in society.

– *Translated by* ANURADHA POTLURI

Notes

1. *Totto-chan, the Little Girl at the Window* – an autobiographical memoir written by Japanese television personality Tetsuko Kuroyanagi, the book was published originally in 1981, and became an instant bestseller in Japan. It was translated into many languages across the world.
2. *mulaqaat* – meeting with family, friends or other visitors, within jail premises, in a designated time slot.
3. *vakalatnama* – a decree/document obtained from a client by a lawyer that authorizes the lawyer to act for and on behalf of the client. A *vakalatnama* may contain general terms or be one with specific terms and conditions to authorize a lawyer to represent the client's matter in any court of law.

Acknowledgements

I had written only a few stories before going to jail. When I shared my thoughts on 'Paro's Children' in one of my letters to Sridhar, another political prisoner in Nagpur jail, he encouraged me to write it up as a story. This paved the way for the jail stories. I am indebted to him but grieve that he did not live to see my stories published in English. I thank Vernon, who inspired me with his own stories, and Arun Ferreira who not only sent me his drawings while I was in prison but also did the illustrations for my stories.

My friend, Vanaja, saw the potential in the experiences I narrated and motivated me to write them down as stories. I wrote one and sent it to the Sunday supplement of the daily newspaper, *Andhra Jyothi*. Vemana Vasanthalakshmi, who was in charge of the Sunday supplement at that time, not only published it but also encouraged me to continue writing and offered to publish them regularly. I thank her and the editor, K. Srinivas.

My friends, Venugopal, Aravinda, Ramky, Ramu, Allam Rajaiah, and Lavanya, read each of my stories before they were sent for publication and gave their frank opinions, enhancing the quality. I am indebted to all of them. I thank all the magazines that published my stories and the Revolutionary Writers Association for publishing them in Telugu as an anthology under the title *Edi Neram?*

I am grateful to Gita Ramaswamy, who came up with the idea of translating my stories into English, and to all the translators. Most of them worked on my stories on Gita's request, even though they did not know me personally. I am grateful to Ratna Books for disseminating my stories among a wider audience by publishing them in English. My heartfelt thanks to everyone who has made this book possible.

ANURADHA BELLAPU

Notes on the Translators

ADITYA K. is a research scholar and a freelance translator. Literature in Indian languages and translation practice deeply interest him. He has translated from English and other languages into Telugu, with some of his major work appearing in the Gauri Lankesh reader in Telugu.

ANURADHA POTLURI studied agriculture but is deeply interested in literature, culture and politics. She reads extensively. This is her first attempt at translation. She lives in Hyderabad.

ARAVINDA POTLURI studied engineering but has a keen interest in literature, economics and politics. She was associated with the Center for Documentation, Research and Communication (CDRC) and *Veekshanam*, a social, political and economic monthly magazine published in Telugu. She is currently studying the intersection of caste and class in India. She lives in Hyderabad.

UTLA BALAJI has worked extensively in the areas of public health and knowledge management, and is a behavioural science expert.

GITA RAMASWAMY is a social activist and writer who works for the Hyderabad Book Trust, a not-for-profit Telugu publishing collective. She has published both in English and Telugu. She has authored *India Stinking: Manual Scavengers in Andhra Pradesh* (Navayana, 2005), and co-authored *Taking Charge of Our Bodies: A Health Handbook for Women* (Penguin, 2004) and *On Their Own* (Otherwise Publications, 2005). She has translated *Ooru, Vaada, Batuku* into English as *Life in Anantharam* (Banyan Tree, 2016). She has edited *Here I Am* (Ratna Books, 2018), an anthology of P. Sathyavathi's stories, and co-edited the *OUP Dalit Anthology of Telugu Literature* (Oxford University Press, 2016).

GORREPATI SAMYUKTHA is a textile designer who works

with handloom weavers in Andhra Pradesh. She is the author of *Learning the Heart Way* (The Other India Books, 2015; Eklavya), a book on her experiences in an experimental higher education programme. She has also authored a few Telugu short stories, some of which have appeared in Telugu dailies. She currently lives in Hyderabad.

RAJ KARAMCHEDU published his first novel, *All Things Unforgiven,* in 2014. He is the publisher of Saaranga Books (www.saarangabooks.com) and Saaranga Magazine (magazine.saarangabooks.com) focusing on Telugu fiction and non-fiction. His translations from Telugu to English have appeared in the anthology, *Here I Am,* by P. Sathyavathi. A selection of Raj's poetry translations appeared in *The Oxford Anthology of Telugu Dalit Poems* (Oxford University Press, 2016). In addition, in October 2014, *The Caravan* magazine published his translations of three Telugu poets: Siva Reddy, Varavara Rao and Ismail.

RIGOBERTHA PRABHATHA has a BEd from the English and Foreign Languages University (EFLU), Hyderabad, and an MA in English Literature from Osmania University. He loves to read books, write reviews and watch films. His translations from Telugu to English have appeared in P. Sathyavathi's anthology, *Here I Am*. Prabhatha works in a publication office.

RATNA MADHAVI is from Delhi. Her sensitivity and passion for literature and languages drew her to writing. She has written poetry, stories for children and adults, and articles, and has been documenting translations in Telugu (her mother tongue), Hindi and English. Having worked as a development professional, a teacher and as an editor, she is now a freelancer and a full-time wordsmith.

M. SASHI KUMAR was born in Hyderabad and is interested in the politics of development, technology and conflict resolution. He has been involved with the not-for-profit sector for over twenty years, before which he worked in the banking industry for a decade.

P. SATHYAVATHI is the author of the award-winning story, 'Glasu Pagilindi', published in 1977. *Illalakagaane*, a volume of short stories, won her the Chaso Award and established her as a leading feminist writer in Telugu. With four novels, five anthologies of short stories, and a volume of essays to her credit, she runs a regular column on the early women writers in *Bhumika*. She has also translated into Telugu, to much acclaim, the works of Ismat Chughtai, A. Revathi's *The Truth About Me: A Hijra Life Story*, Y.B. Satyanarayana's *My Father Baliah*, C.K. Janu's *Mother Earth* and Paula Richman's *The Many Ramayanas: The Diversity of a Narrative Tradition in South Asia*. Having retired as an English lecturer, she now lives in Vijayawada.

SUDHA KIRAN works in the software industry. He is a writer, translator and an analyst. He has published poems and articles on several aspects of literature, economy, politics and trends in the IT industry in various magazines.

SUDHAKAR UNUDURTI is a marine engineer by profession. His interest in maritime history led him to write short stories in Telugu. *Toorupu Gaalulu*, an anthology of his short stories that fictionalized the history of the coastal Andhra region, received critical acclaim. He has also translated an article by Gauri Lankesh, which was included in the Telugu anthology of her writings.

SUREKHA AITABATHULA was born in Yanam and raised in Hyderabad. She has a postgraduate degree in English Literature and a postgraduate degree in Journalism and Communication from Osmania University, as also in counselling psychology from the Hyderabad Academy of Psychology. She works in the Doordarshan Kendra, Hyderabad. This is her first attempt at a formal translation.

N. VENUGOPAL is a poet, literary critic, journalist, translator and public speaker. Born and educated in Warangal, he has been associated since his early teens with *Srjana*, a leading Telugu journal for modern literature. He has been writing and translating for the past four decades. He has published more than twenty-five books in Telugu and translated as many from English. He currently edits *Veekshanam*, an alternative monthly journal on political economy and society.

About the Author

B. Anuradha is a women's rights activist based in Hyderabad. While working for a bank in Hyderabad, she came in contact with the Andhra Pradesh Civil Liberties Committee and worked as an activist from 1990 to 1993 and later as a women's rights activist. She resigned from her job in 1996 to work in the Chaitanya Mahila Sangam, a state-wide women's organization. She was on the editorial board of the magazine, *Mahila Margam*. In 2005, she relocated to Jharkhand to work as an activist in the Nari Mukti Sangh. She was arrested in October 2009 and spent four years in the Hazaribagh Central Jail.

Anuradha has written twenty-seven short stories and several articles. Most of her prison stories have been published in the Sunday special edition of the daily *Andhra Jyothi*, as well as in *Mahila Margam*, *Aruna Tara*, *Sahithi Godavari* and the web magazine, *Saranga*. Sixteen of these stories were later published as a collection by Virasam (Revolutionary Writers Association). Some of the stories were also translated into Hindi and published in Hindi magazines. 'Paro's Children' was translated into Bengali.

She has translated *The Prisons We Broke* by Baby Kamble, *Articles of Ambedkar on Women (Feminist Ambedkar)*, and *Feminising the Labour Relations* by Dr M. Vanamala into Telugu, and co-translated Frantz Fanon's *The Wretched of the Earth* along with N. Ravi.

About the Author

About the Editor

Gita Ramaswamy works with the Hyderabad Book Trust, a not-for-profit Telugu publishing collective. She has co-authored *Taking Charge of Our Bodies* (Penguin, 2004), *On Their Own* (Otherwise Publications, 2004), *The Oxford University Press Anthology of Telugu Dalit Literature* (Oxford University Press, 2016) and has authored *India Stinking* (Navayana, 2005). She also translates from Telugu to English and has translated the book *Life in Anantharam* (Banyan Tree, 2016).

The HarperCollins–Ratna Sagar Translation Series

Ratna Sagar is an Indian publishing company founded in 1982; Ratna Books, its translations-only imprint, was launched in 2017. The aim of the Ratna Sagar translation list has been to bring acclaimed works written in the Indian languages to a wider readership in English translation, and the focus has been to ensure the quality of the translations, to provide the reader with a seamless reading experience.

Forty-two books have been published in the Ratna Sagar translation list so far, all in hardback. The books have been received well by readers and have met with critical acclaim from the media; many of the books have also won or been nominated for literary awards.

HarperCollins is proud to partner with Ratna Sagar to bring this list of high-quality translations to readers in paperback editions, publishing under HarperCollins's prestigious Perennial imprint.

READ MORE

Havan by Mallikarjun Hiremath

Leaf, Water and Flow by Avadhoot Dongare

Parthiban's Dream by Kalki Krishnamurthy

Prison Notes of a Woman Activist by Bellapu Anuradha

The Bells Are Ringing in Haridwar by M. Mukundan

Dukhi Dadiba by Dadi Edulji Taraporewala

After Yesterday and Other Stories by Appaduari Muttulingam

The Sixth Finger by Malayatoor Ramakrishnan

A Faceless Evening and Other Stories by Gangadhar Gadgil

If a River and Other Stories by Kula Saikia

On a River's Bank by A. Madhavan

Echoes of the Veena and Other Stories by R. Chudamani

Here I Am and Other Stories by P. Sathyavathi

The Rock That Was Not and Other Stories by Githanjali

The Story of Being Useless and Three Contexts of a Writer by Avadhoot Dongare

Mirror in the Hall and Other Stories by Prakash Bal Joshi

The Songs of Life and Other Stories by Vijaya Rajadhyaksha

Jalasamadhi and Other Stories by A. Sethumadhavan

Kadambari - The Flower Girl by A. Sethumadhavan

The Scent of Happiness by R. Vatsala

Asprishya Ganga and Other Stories by Kolakaluri Enoch

Alka and Other Stories by Goutam Das

If there is a God and Other Stories by Imayam

Ananta Jeevanam by Kolakaluri Enoch

The Stepmother and Other Stories by Laxmibai Abhyankar

Cracked Glass Jar and Other Stories by Chandra Latha

A Fine Thread and Other Stories by B. Jeyamohan

Forever Yours, Krishna by Indira Parthasarathy

Mayaloka by Poornachandra Tejaswi

The Go-Between and Other Stories by Ghanshyam Desai

The Masked Face and Two Other Stories by Vaasanthi

Vasudeva ... The Wanderer Prince by Sanghadasagani Vacaka

Randhi: Of Power and Desire by Kolakaluri Enoch

HarperCollins *Publishers* India

At HarperCollins India, we believe in telling the best stories and finding the widest readership for our books in every format possible. We started publishing in 1992; a great deal has changed since then, but what has remained constant is the passion with which our authors write their books, the love with which readers receive them, and the sheer joy and excitement that we as publishers feel in being a part of the publishing process.

Over the years, we've had the pleasure of publishing some of the finest writing from the subcontinent and around the world, including several award-winning titles and some of the biggest bestsellers in India's publishing history. But nothing has meant more to us than the fact that millions of people have read the books we published, and that somewhere, a book of ours might have made a difference.

As we look to the future, we go back to that one word—a word which has been a driving force for us all these years.

Read.